Magdalena Gottschalk:

The Slippery Slope

M. Gail Grant

~ DEDICATION ~

Tomorrow is never promised, and today is a gift. Live life to its fullest and have no regrets. To all my friends and family, I am blessed you are a part of my life. As the sun rises and sets, I thank God for this life and His many blessings.

~ M. Gail Grant

~ AUTHOR'S NOTE ~

This book is a work of fiction. Names, characters, places, and events are all a product of the author's imagination or have been used in a fictitious nature. Any resemblance or link to actual people (living or deceased), places, or events, is coincidental in nature and does not represent the author's intent.

* 2018 NYC Big Book Award Winner: Category: Juvenile Fiction

https://www.nycbigbookaward.com/2018winners

Readers' Favorite 5 – Star Review:

https://readersfavorite.com/book-review/magdalena-gottschalk/1

"Grant's world of Lily Brooke and the Enchanted Forest is inspired, especially when seen in contrast, as the bucolic little town is such a difference from the supernatural world the forest represents. This story also works quite well as a coming of age tale as each of the characters adapts to the seriousness of their situation and masters fear and insecurity to help the other MALB teammates. Grant's plot is sound and great fun to follow, and her characters are well-defined. Magdalena

Gottschalk: The Slippery Slope is most highly recommended."

~ J. Magnus, Readers' Favorite Reviewer

"The eye-catching cover complements the story and Grant's prose is as charming as ever. The narrative is vivid, the dialogue is clean, and the moderate pace suits the plot well."

~ L. Amri, Readers' Favorite Reviewer

"By chapter four the reader is thrown into an action-packed adventure with this group of friends. It was a good story and I think that it could be very well received in the pre-teen age group. If this was available in my 12 year-old son's school library, I'm sure it would be one that he would want to read."

~ D. Sweeney, Readers' Favorite Reviewer

~ABOUT THE AUTHOR~

Writing has always been my underlying passion in life. I hold a Bachelor of Science degree in Psychology and a formal minor in Sociology, as I felt understanding and studying human behavior on both the individual and collective levels would enhance anything and everything that I chose to do in life. Currently, I am a second-year graduate teaching assistant in the Master of Arts in Professional Writing program for English Composition at Kennesaw State University.

The desire to write has always been an integral part of who I am, and as my father's health began to decline, I decided it was time to seize the moment. Placing the rough-draft manuscript for book #1 of the **Magdalena Gottschalk** series in his hands was one of life's most precious moments. I attended a summer literary writer's camp around age twelve. Having cherished every moment of the experience, these childhood influences are found in MALB's many adventures.

I have always been an avid reader of books from intense young adult thrillers to light-hearted summer romances. During middle school summers, I used to stay up to the wee hours of the morning reading because I just couldn't put the book down.

This basic idea, not being able to put a book down, is the principal I have built upon while composing this middle-grade fantasy thriller series. It has moments of ease, moments of intensity, moments of spiritual exploration, and moments of humor, all the while encapsulating a paranormal and fantastical world. I have strived to collaboratively portray excitement and innocence of coming of age paradigms along with elements of faith woven through the underpinnings.

Hope, teamwork, friendship, and embracing differences are realistic components of life that MALB must face. There is a time for sweetness, a time for seriousness, and always a time for kindness and life lessons.

~M. Gail

~ CONTENTS ~

HOLIDAY CELEBRATION

~ One ~

Magdalena sat on the park bench underneath the twinkling white lights, amazed at the sight before her. The holidays always brought such a sense of nostalgia for her, and after everything she had been through this past fall, well with the demons and all, she felt even more thankful this holiday season for the friends and family that surrounded her.

No more, she thought.

No more will she ever take for granted the blessings of each day. From sunrise to sunset, she would try to remember how blessed she was to simply exist in the special, quaint town of Lily Brooke.

It wasn't that long ago, Magdalena had thought her life was missing something profound. She smiled fondly as the memories of her thirteenth birthday came flooding back to her. September twenty-fifth, her special day, had been frocked with excitement, friends, family, and oh, that yummy chocolate cake. Well, that wasn't to mention the

Fleischsalat sandwiches that she had helped her mother, Leona Gottschalk, make the evening before. They were her absolute favorite and made her birthday celebration just perfect.

Remembering that late autumn day, Magdalena couldn't help but feel a sense of guilt well up within her. She remembered standing over her birthday cake with all thirteen candles lit, praying for something big and exciting to come her way. She had grown up with a sense of longing and felt she had a purpose that was yet to be identified. The small-town feel of Lily Brooke, although something she now welcomed with open arms, sometimes seemed to smother her soul. She had thought she was bigger than the life she had lived up to her first teenage years.

Well, as karma would have it, something had come along not long after her amazing birthday celebration to help her put things into perspective very quickly. No longer did she hope for the chaos and excitement of the unknown. These days, she reveled in the calmness and predictability of knowing the demons were still locked up inside of the enchanted lanterns.

Sitting there on the park bench with her mind a million miles away, Magdalena still couldn't believe everything that had happened over that late fall weekend. Here she sat, three months later, and the anxiety was still bottled up inside of her. She felt chills every morning when she sat up in bed to swing her legs around, meeting her pink, fuzzy bedroom slippers on the floor beside her bed. It wasn't that long ago she had woken up in night sweats, her pajamas missing, and her muddy running shoes sitting by her bed. She could still smell the evil breath of the Grand Demon as he mocked her, letting her know he had been responsible for her tantalizing nightmares.

Shivering, Magdalena wasn't sure if it was due to the memories and thoughts running through her mind this evening, or the outdoor cold temperature this time of year. Silently, she was hoping it was the freezing air because the thought of being manipulated still to this day by the demons, was something that really didn't make her proud. The memories from that autumn weekend would last the rest of her life, and she had no doubt.

Time seemed to stand still as Magdalena sat on the park bench, watching the young children laugh and play. Determined to enjoy her favorite time of year, she pushed the hurtful memories of last fall to the back of her mind the best she could. The demons had been beaten and restrained for eternity, she hoped. But, the lasting effects of the mind games would always be a part of her soul going forward. However, she was not about to let those treacherous memories steal her joy during this festive time of the season. As she sat willfully enjoying the serenity of the moment, she noticed Gabriel approaching her.

Walking with his head down, hands in his pockets, which happened to be Gabriel's style, he had caught sight of Magdalena sitting on the park bench underneath the twinkling lights. He was so excited to see his best friend out and about, not sitting in her bedroom at home alone. He knew this past autumn had been very difficult for her and knew she had needed time for herself to heal. He realized her life had changed so quickly on the turn of a dime. He was just thrilled to see her beginning to come out of the shell she had built around herself these last three months. It saddened him so very much to see her in pain.

"Hi, Mags! It is so good to see you. Have you been here long?" asked Gabriel.

He took a seat beside his best friend since Kindergarten.

"Hi, Gabriel! So good to see you, too! No, I've been here for a few minutes but was just taking in the scene of all the children enjoying the moment. How have you been?" asked Magdalena.

"Good! I've been missing our adventures, of course, but I have been keeping busy helping my dad in his blacksmith shop. He stays so busy now almost year-round, which is great. I guess, especially this time of year, everyone is ordering iron gates for gifts," replied Gabriel.

"Yes, I bet they are! He is so talented. So glad to hear he is keeping busy and you, too," said Magdalena. "I must admit, though, I have missed our walks and talks these last few months. I have been so preoccupied with all of the life changes that I'm sorry I haven't made more time for the rest of the gang and us. I haven't spent any time with Hubert, Cody, Piper, or Greta since that night. I mean, I see them at school in passing, but, well, you know what I mean."

Gabriel leaned over and gave Magdalena a warm hug. He had truly missed her presence and knew there wasn't much he could say that would heal her pain. Only time would give her the mental clarity she needed to accept her future. But one thing was for sure, he would be there when she was ready to move forward. Witch or no witch, she was his favorite friend.

Magdalena felt Gabriel's warm embrace, and before she knew it, for no apparent reason, the tears began to fall down her face softly. She had been resisting the new-found revelation of being a witch ever since that fateful night. Thinking she was doing better, she had decided to venture out and partake in the holiday festivities. But, seeing Gabriel and feeling his arms wrapped around her made her realize maybe she wasn't as healed as she had hoped.

Gabriel noticed the tears, and before he thought, he softly wiped them away. He stared into her eyes, seeing the pain well up beneath those beautiful green windows to her soul.

"I'm so sorry, Gabriel. I haven't had any time with you for months, and here I sit crying. This is ridiculous!"

"No, it isn't ridiculous, Mags. You need to allow yourself time to accept your feelings. To move forward, you must deal with the healing process and embrace the change. No matter what, I am here for you. Tears don't bother me!" exclaimed Gabriel.

That brought a giggle to Magdalena, and she understood now why Gabriel had always been such an important part of her life.

"Well, no more tears or sadness! This is my favorite time of the year, and we must enjoy the seasonal festivities!" laughed Magdalena.

"Amen, to that!" shouted Gabriel.

As the two friends sat on the park bench underneath the twinkling Christmas lights watching the children play, light snow began to fall. Magdalena and Gabriel closed their eyes and felt the fresh white powder upon their noses and cheeks. Once again, Magdalena remembered what it was like to feel carefree and happy. Gabriel had a way of always making that happen for her.

Daylight was dwindling, and off in the distance, they could hear the community of Lily Brooke coming together as the Christmas carols had begun. The harmony of all the voices singing together in traditional songs of the season was like food for Magdalena's soul.

Ah, she thought.

This was what it was like to live in a moment and just let go. Let go of the past, let go of the pain, let go of the disappointment.

As she opened her eyes, Magdalena noticed some of the children had gathered around the center of the park and began singing Christmas carols of their own, while playing ring around the rosies, or something that appeared similar in nature. They were holding hands, giggling, and running around in one large circle singing at the top of their lungs.

With a smile, Magdalena turned to Gabriel and said, "How about we go join them?"

Gabriel smiled back, knowing this was about to be one of the best evenings of his life, grabbed Magdalena's hand, and off they went to sing, skip, and play. Being thirteen allowed them the freedom to be young adults when they chose or to be children when they wanted. And right now, with the softly falling snow, twinkling lights, and carols being sung by many, the choice wasn't a difficult one.

Around and around they went, falling to the ground in dizziness while laughing harder than Magdalena had ever remembered doing before. This was what her life purpose entailed. Being a witch had nothing to do with how she lived her life. It was a reality, yes. But, it was completely up to her how she allowed it to control her thoughts and actions. *And, from this day forward*, she thought, *it was no longer important.* Friends and family were what she would live for and well, maybe an adventure in the future. But right now, she had lived enough adventure for a lifetime.

M. Gail Grant

CHRISTMAS IN LILY BROOKE

~ Two ~

Having had one of the best evenings in a very long time, Magdalena remembered how much she loved life and how the simple things were often found at the heart of living. Laughing, singing, dancing in the snow, and celebrating the holiday season was just what she had needed. Add in Gabriel's company, and well, it was the perfect evening. She realized how much she missed the rest of her friends after watching all the children play together. Gabriel had thought it would be a great idea to have everyone get together since they hadn't seen each other since that fateful night. Magdalena had agreed, so Gabriel was going to contact everyone and have them all meet at the old tire swing later that evening.

She would be lying if she didn't admit the thought of being at that tree again made her shiver, but before that horrific night, some of her absolute best life experiences had been spent swinging on that old tire swing. So, as reluctant as she was to go, she knew it was something she needed to do to put the effects of the past behind her. At five o'clock that evening, she would be back with her long, lost friends.

MALB, the Mystical Alliance of Lily Brooke, would reconvene where it had all originally begun. The childhood memories began flooding back to Magdalena as she stood lost in thought. Even back then, Gabriel used to chase her around that old oak tree.

The group, MALB, would divide into two teams, calling themselves the royals and the robbers, and bring on the best games of hiding go seek ever! They had so much fun that neither team cared who did the hiding and who did the seeking. The robbers were trying to steal from the royals, and they could never remember who was a royal and who was a robber.

Magdalena giggled to herself, thinking about how they must have looked being so engaged in their roles back in the day. The hardest part of life was when it turned dark outside, and you could hear the moms shouting to their children to get home. It was something they had most definitely taken for granted. She knew the minute she saw a firefly that she had better get to running, for the wrath of Leona Gottschalk could be severe. Even though she never raised her voice much, when she did, you could see the fury in her eyes.

Magdalena gave a light shudder as she now realized her mother was an enchanted witch. *What she could have done to discipline Allison and herself if she had chosen to do so would be quite awful*, thought Magdalena.

The Mystical Alliance of Lily Brooke had been together since those early Kindergarten years. The idea of having a secret club amongst the six of them was so enticing. However, once they would meet at the tire swing, they realized they didn't have any real mysteries to solve. So, with their creative imaginations and all, they made up so-called mysteries that needed to be solved in the best interest of Lily Brooke. After a few hours, though, it often ended in the royals and robbers chasing each other.

Oh, the good old days, thought Magdalena.

"Magdalena!" shouted Allison. "What are you doing just standing there staring at the grapevines? You look possessed," laughed little Allison.

Magdalena had to giggle a little, too, because as lost in thought as she had been, she knew she appeared to be a little spacey.

"Hi, little sis, how are you this morning? I was thinking about when I was your age and how much fun I used to have with my friends," responded Magdalena.

"I see, did you go to the town Christmas carols last night? I didn't see you there. But, I didn't leave the hot chocolate cart much, either. Mom and dad were busy chatting with everyone, so I took the opportunity to have a few cups of the yummy, candy cane hot chocolate, that Adolphe made," smirked Allison.

Magdalena walked over to where her favorite little person stood and gave her one of those bear hugs that squeezed the breath out of you. Allison, even with a six-year age gap between them, was such an important part of Magdalena's life. She had always treasured her relationship with her little sister, but now that Magdalena knew for sure that she was indeed a witch, they had grown even closer.

There was a fifty-fifty chance that possibly one day, Allison would discover she may also be a witch. It was too early to tell since the gift of spiritual hearing, the first tell-tell sign of enchantment, typically didn't manifest itself until young adulthood. Magdalena was the second child of her age that had discovered the ability of spiritual hearing.

And, with that discovery, she knew the trials, thoughts, and emotions that one day, her baby sister might endure. But then again, Magdalena had discovered her father was a pure human even though her mother was a witch. So, if Allison were lucky, she would also be a pure human. Until that day arrived, Magdalena had every intention of keeping a watchful eye on her little sister.

"I can't breathe! You are squeezing the life out of me!" exclaimed Allison.

She gently pulled away from Magdalena and took a big gasp of air to refill her lungs.

"Geez Magdalena, you have like super-human strength," smiled Allison.

"Oh, sorry little sis, I just got so excited hugging you. I didn't mean to hurt you," replied Magdalena.

Allison saw the genuine concern in Magdalena's eyes and replied, "It's okay! I still love you, anyway."

"I promise I won't tell mom about all the hot chocolate you drank last night," laughed Magdalena.

She knew how intense Allison's love of sweets was, and she knew how she would do just about anything to sneak sugar. Why, Allison had almost dove into Magdalena's four-tier chocolate birthday cake, before Leona Gottschalk had caught and scolded her.

"Oh, thank you, sissy! You know mom, she would seriously be upset with me," said Allison.

"Upset with you for what?" inquired Leona Gottschalk.

Magdalena and Allison looked up and realized their mother had stealthily appeared from nowhere onto the patio. *Uh oh*, they thought, hoping Leona hadn't heard much more of their conversation.

"Oh, nothing, mom. I was just kidding," sang Allison while she quickly skipped towards the back door.

She figured it was time to abruptly exit before her mother decided to ask any additional questions about the conversation she had just happened upon between the sisters.

As Allison exited the patio, Leona gave Magdalena one of those mom all-knowing grins.

"I saw her visiting Adolphe's hot chocolate cart several times yesterday evening while we were enjoying the celebration at the town square," stated Leona. "She thinks we didn't notice, but Adolphe seemed so pleased with his specialty cart of toppings that I didn't have the heart to catch her in the act and stop the fun. I do remember how good whipped cream, cinnamon, and candy canes are when added to hot chocolate!" exclaimed Leona.

With that, both Magdalena and her mother broke into hysterical laughter as the holidays tended to bring out the child in everyone.

"So, what do you have on the agenda today, Magdalena?" asked Leona.

Secretly, she noticed Magdalena had finally started to leave the house again and had even spent the past evening with Gabriel. She didn't know why, but the last few months, Magdalena seemed to have withdrawn and stayed much to herself. She really hoped nothing had happened between the two of them to cause a ripple in their friendship. They had been friends for such a long time and had grown up together, she mused. It would break her heart to see them lose that bond.

"Well, I ran into Gabriel last night at the town celebration, and we decided to get together with the rest of the gang this evening. As far as the day goes, I can help you wrap gifts or finish any last-minute Christmas shopping!" replied Magdalena excitedly.

Magdalena couldn't help but hope that maybe she got to wrap some of her own gifts, which may allow for just a little pre-Christmas peeking.

"That sounds great! I have a stack of gifts that you can wrap for me. I will pull everything together and set it up in the kitchen on the table. Your father is taking Allison to her ballet rehearsal so she won't be around to spy," smiled Leona.

"Sounds good, mother."

Leona left to pull everything together and make sure that Allison was ready to leave for rehearsal. This was going to be Allison's first year performing in the Lily Brooke Christmas ballet. And if she were honest with herself, Leona absolutely couldn't wait to watch her daughter perform on stage. Growing up without the opportunity to do these types of things made Leona appreciate the experiences with her children even more.

Magdalena watched her mother hurriedly run back into the house, and once again, she found herself alone. Christmas was only a week away, and she was bursting with excitement. It had been such a long, few months that she was ready to embrace the spirit of the season. This year, she knew she had much in which to be thankful. Things could have turned out very differently when the demons had taken it upon themselves to try and steal the golden leaf, the power of all power in Lily Brooke.

Taking one last glance at the coveted vine-covered patio, Magdalena reminisced about her favorite childhood past-times a few minutes longer and went inside to find the scent of warm, apple streusel in the oven. Oh, yum, *my mom is the best*, she knew.

Paulos Gottschalk, the patriarchal head of the household, was running out the door with his little ballerina yelling, "Good morning, Magdalena! Sorry honey, running out the door, but I hope you have an amazing day!"

Magdalena laughed, "It's okay, dad. Don't be late!"

And with that, Magdalena heard the front door slam.

Gabriel had spent all morning out and about visiting with friends, letting everyone know that MALB would be getting together that evening by meeting at the old tire swing. So far, Hubert, Greta, and Piper had confirmed they would be there and were excited to see everyone. He just needed to speak with Cody, and then they should all be good to go.

Realizing how hungry he was, Gabriel noticed the seasonal smells coming from Adolphe's bakery as he was heading down Rownalt Street towards Cody's house.

Hmm, he thought. Maybe I will slip into Adolphe's and grab a late breakfast pastry quickly.

He had been so excited about getting the gang back together, that he had forgotten to eat breakfast earlier this morning. As Gabriel opened the door, he heard the little bell letting Adolphe know someone had just entered the shop.

There came the town's baker, running from the back kitchen with his white apron and chef's hat attire. Adolphe kindly smiled as soon as he saw Gabriel, even though he knew he must look a fright covered in flour from head to toe.

"What can I do for you, Gabriel?" inquired Adolphe.

"Gee, I don't know, Adolphe. Everything looks and smells so good; I can't decide!" exclaimed Gabriel.

Hearing this, Adolphe gave a little joyful laugh. He lived to hear those very words. Baking was his passion, and it showed. Every celebration in Lily Brooke that was a celebration at all, featured Adolphe's food creations.

"Well, Gabriel, I have a new recipe that I'm testing this morning. It is a blend of cinnamon, apple, and maple, and is topped with chopped walnuts. Oh, and I should mention it is an over-sized donut. I'm calling it autumn maple donut. Want to give it a try?"

"Oh, my, Adolphe! Yes!" shouted Gabriel.

I mean, how could I not try that, he thought.

Adolphe was obviously pleased with Gabriel's decision and ran to the back of the kitchen, returning with the first sample of his new recipe.

Gabriel dug into his pocket to pull out a dollar to pay Adolphe. But when Adolphe realized what Gabriel was doing, he exclaimed, "Oh, no, no, no! This is on me. Let me know how it tastes."

Gabriel reached out and took the warm, massively large donut, which seemed to be closer to the size of a small pizza, and sampled the first bite.

An explosion of flavor rocked Gabriel's senses as he tasted the warm goodness. He could almost feel his eyes rolling into the back of his head. The apple, the cinnamon, the maple, the walnut; It was the absolute perfect blend of autumn goodness.

Apparently, Adolphe's nerves were on edge because before Gabriel could even swallow the bite, he heard, "Well? What do you think? Is it okay to add to the glass showcase, or does it need more work?"

Gabriel choked down the donut bite and said, "Adolphe, you have out-done yourself, yet again! This is fantastic. I believe this is my new favorite; the flavors blend perfectly together."

Adolphe looked like he was going to cry. He had worked nonstop for days trying to perfect this new recipe.

"Why, thank you, Gabriel. I'm so glad you like it!"

Before Gabriel could respond, the little bakery door opened, and Adolphe had to move on to the next customer. Gabriel waved goodbye and turned down Rownalt Street, again heading toward Cody's house.

He smiled to himself because he had such treasured memories of coming to Adolphe's on Saturday mornings with his dad when he was younger. Adolphe always seemed to have a new recipe for them to try. And quite honestly, it was always just absolutely amazing. Gabriel missed those days, but he was happy that his dad's business was growing, keeping him in the blacksmith shop on the weekends. As talented as Mr. Bach was in making the wrought iron gates, it didn't surprise him much.

But, as much as Gabriel loved his dad, he missed his mother deeply. He had never known her as she had passed away right after childbirth. She often visited Gabriel in his sleep, he knew. When he awakened, her presence could always be felt. It was a secret he had told no one, not even Magdalena, because it was so special to him. Her photograph sat on his bedside table, making it the first thing he saw each morning as he awoke.

Gabriel turned down the street where Cody lived and saw him outside on the lawn with a puppy.

Interesting, thought Gabriel. He didn't remember Cody having a dog.

As Gabriel approached, the puppy and Cody noticed his presence, and all chaos ensued. The puppy decided Gabriel looked like some type of a human chew toy.

"Oh, no," grumbled Cody. "Mac, stop!"

The little two-toned beagle was pulling on Gabriel's pant leg with fierce determination. Apparently, Gabriel's leg was looking quite tasty.

Gabriel laughed at the little pup's tenacity. He was so tiny that Gabriel knew if Mac were strong enough for his sharp teeth to find Gabriel's skin, it wouldn't do much damage. Meanwhile, Cody continued to scold the energetic pup while trying to pry his teeth out of Gabriel's pant leg.

"I didn't know that you had a puppy," said Gabriel.

"Well, I just got him yesterday. As you can see, he doesn't even know his name yet, but he will come around; I hope."

Laughing, Gabriel said, "Oh, he is just a pup! I'm sure he will come along, just fine."

Bending down, Gabriel helped Cody remove the feisty canine from his leg while petting the top of Mac's head. With the two of them working together, Mac was safely removed, teeth and all. Cody decided to hold him in lieu of letting him run around, which would evidently just cause more ruckus.

"What brings you around today?" asked Cody.

"I saw Mags last night. She mentioned it had been quite a while since we all got together. She's right! It has been too long. So, everyone is meeting at the old oak tree this evening at five o'clock. We are hoping you don't already have plans and can go," replied Gabriel.

"That sounds fantastic!" exclaimed Cody. "I've been so bored lately. I think we all needed a little time to recover from our last adventure," laughed Cody. "It isn't every day you go to battle with demons."

"Amen to that," mumbled Gabriel. "Thank goodness."

Cody could hear his mother calling, probably wondering where the little terror of a dog was, so he excused himself from Gabriel but promising to be at the tire swing at five o'clock sharp.

Gabriel waved goodbye and headed back home to see if his dad could use some help in the shop over the next few hours. He had become quite fond of their time spent working together.

The afternoon seemed to go by quickly for all as MALB was equally excited about their reunion. Each of them couldn't wait to enjoy spending time together and just having fun. This time they wouldn't be traipsing through sacrificial caves, touring enchanted treehouses, and running from demons.

Tonight, it was going to be an opportunity for all of them to enjoy each other's company and do what children do best, play! Well, at their age, maybe hang out would be a more appropriate description.

This time of year, daylight was low on the horizon by four-thirty in the afternoon. Gabriel didn't have far to go as the old oak tree and tire swing were hidden in the woods back behind his father's blacksmith shop. He bid his dad goodbye and headed towards the rendezvous about four-forty-five p.m.

The air was brisk, and the newly fallen snow gave a pure, fresh smell to the air. He was so excited for the gathering that it took almost everything he had not to skip along the way. Carrying his rolled-up sleeping bag and extra blankets for warmth, he secretly felt like a little kid on Christmas morning.

As Gabriel came upon the old oak tree, he realized everyone else had already arrived. Magdalena stood chatting with the group, and everyone seemed equally thrilled to be back together. Gabriel's heart skipped a little beat as the comforting memories of the past resurfaced.

"Hi, Gabriel! This was such a great idea!" exclaimed Greta. "I didn't realize how much I have missed the gang."

"Yeah, man! This is just like old times! Tonight, we aren't here to chase demons. We are here to have fun," announced Hubert. "Like, dudes, no more of that stuff for me. It took me weeks to sleep without a light on after our last adventure. And, probably even longer than that to go back inside my own barn."

The rest of the gang laughed hysterically at Hubert. Somehow, he always seemed to find the bluntest of words to express what everyone else was thinking.

What made Hubert different, thought Gabriel, *was he had no filter.* If Hubert thought it, Hubert said it; period. There was nothing in between.

"Guess what I brought, guys?" Magdalena had that sly smile while waiting on her friends to guess.

"I sure hope it isn't something gold in the shape of a leaf," mumbled Hubert. "Or, something that looks like a jewelry box engraved with antique gold and gems."

"No, silly!"

Magdalena had a pain shoot through her core for a moment, as Hubert's words brought back that night. The engraved box had held and protected the golden leaf, the key to the highest power found in all of Lily Brooke. Had they not have found that box under the water deep within the sacrificial cave, they wouldn't have ever been able to defeat the three enchanted demons.

Magdalena could feel the cold shivers running up and down her spine. The engraved golden leaf paired with the lily root had saved their lives. Black magic had saved their community, and as much as they would all love to forget, it was their new-found reality.

"Well, what did you bring, Magdalena? Don't keep us in suspense," replied Gabriel.

Magdalena snapped back to the present and dug from underneath her pink winter coat, strands of Christmas lights.

"How fun!" shouted Greta. "Where do you want to hang them?"

"Well, I thought where better to celebrate the holidays together than our childhood meeting spot?" answered Magdalena.

"Wow, what a great idea! Let's do this," replied Piper. Now, even he was excited.

The six friends worked tirelessly together, and before they knew it, the old oak tree and tire swing were lit up in the colors of the season. Whoever had invented battery-operated Christmas lights had earned the genius award as far as MALB was concerned.

For the next several hours, the friends took turns pushing each other on the festive tire swing, sat in the old oak tree chatting about life, and roasted smores over an open campfire that Cody and Piper built. Hubert, of course, had come tonight prepared with food. Well, if truth be known, it had been his mother's idea when she heard the gang was going camping for the night behind Otis Bach's shop. Yes, Mrs. Mueller was kind and thoughtful in that way. She was always keeping Hubert fed; well, he was always hungry.

Magdalena stole a private moment, just taking in the scene around her. These were the people she loved and adored, and she wouldn't change this moment for the world. The laughter she witnessed was light and genuine. The moment was storybook perfect; the amber glow from the campfire was so warm and inviting.

It was getting late, and everyone was full of chocolate, graham crackers, and marshmallows. Smores had been the ultimate topping to a perfect night in the woods. Everyone now gathered around the campfire, snuggled tight in their sleeping bags and began telling ghost stories. Well, it wasn't a camping trip without ghost stories, even though these days the stories seemed a little eerier than they had before last fall's adventures.

Cody couldn't help but glance over at the side of the oak tree where he had witnessed the worst words he had ever seen carved into a tree. It had read, 'MALB will die.' His blood felt like liquid steel running through his veins as he remembered that moment when his life had flashed in front of his eyes. Now, he knew it had simply been the demons taunting them. But, the memories were intense, nonetheless.

Magdalena noticed Cody's gaze at the tree and watched the emotions play out on his face. She said nothing but could read his every thought and wished there was a way to fix his pain. It was all now history, and each person had to find a way to deal with it in their own way.

For her, it had been seclusion. For the others, it had been companionship and avoidance. As the ghost stories continued, Magdalena found herself drifting to sleep with the nostalgic memories of the old oak tree and tire swing as comfort. Even though turning thirteen had been an event that she couldn't seem to wait for, she now knew in the deepest place of her heart, childhood innocence was to be treasured as it truly doesn't last forever.

THE SLIPPERY SLOPE

~ Three ~

Completely startled, Magdalena opened her eyes and lie completely still.

Had she been dreaming? She wondered.

Lying so still that she wasn't even sure she was breathing in oxygen, she listened intently for what may have awakened her.

It seemed like hours went by, but Magdalena knew all too well that anxiety and anticipation would speed things up in the mind. She couldn't have been lying there awake for more than a moment or two, tops.

Glancing around, Magdalena saw the rest of her friends sleeping soundly, tucked tightly into their sleeping bags. The campfire everyone had enjoyed was now a soft glow, barely hanging on while providing just enough warmth for all to appear comfortable.

Magdalena was dressed warmly for the occasion, so she knew the shivering that she was experiencing had nothing to do with the cold temperatures, and everything to do with her nerves.

Typically, she wasn't so jumpy. But, something about coming face to face with a demon trying to strangle the life out of you had seemed to change things, just a bit.

Magdalena decided the best thing to do would be to roll over and try and go back to sleep. Lord knew she wasn't about to get out of that sleeping bag and explore anything by herself.

Those days were long gone, she thought. Then suddenly, she heard it again.

Heart pounding through her chest, Magdalena realized the sound she had just heard was the same thing that had woken her up moments ago. Instantly knowing what it was, she lay there with eyes closed, praying that God would intervene, and somehow she would wake up in her comfy and cozy bed, making this all a dream. But, the longer she lay there, the more aware she was that this most certainly was not a dream.

She had read about werewolves in the golden leaf book and had known unbeknownst to many, they really did exist. She assumed they probably trolled the woods surrounding Lily Brooke, given its enchanted past. But, she had eased her mind just enough to believe there wasn't any reason that she needed to know for sure. The demons were locked back up into the enchanted lanterns, so all should be safe and sound.

Why would there still be werewolves prowling the woods? she wondered.

Maybe, they were lost.

Legend presented that werewolves hide from humans and don't want to be discovered. They are known by those involved with dark magic, but not to pure humans.

And, then, a terrible thought struck her mind. It had been several months since that fateful night last autumn. Since then, all demonic activity in Lily Brooke had disappeared. But, if werewolves really were protectors of the demons, as she had read, who were feeding them?

Magdalena could feel her stomach begin to flip flop and tried her best to calm her nerves.

Hungry werewolves, that was not a sight she wanted to see. Better yet, not a sight she wanted to think about at all.

Then, it occurred to her; why was she the only one awake?

Not again, she thought. *Lord, please let the others hear the werewolves, and not just her!*

Magdalena had to fight back the tears with everything she possessed. Her mind, body, and spirit were not ready to battle anything demonic, again. And she probably never would!

She lay there, racking her brain, trying to remember everything she had recently read about the evil creatures. The only tidbit she could remember was they are gatekeepers to the demons, a watchful and protective eye over the enchanted woods, that only came out at night. She knew their loyalty would be to their demon leaders, and she knew that thanks to MALB, the three demon leaders were now living eternity inside of a lantern; three separate lanterns, to be exact.

Knowing that ultimately she would have to face the werewolves, Magdalena slowly and quietly exited the sleeping bag. A sense of dread that surrounded Magdalena was almost more than she could bear. This was the last thing she was prepared for, as the golden leaf was locked up inside of the jeweled box, hidden away for safekeeping. She knew she wasn't completely powerless, as hidden underneath her layers of clothing hung the locket with lily root inside. She never went anywhere without it.

Never again, she thought.

Lily root saved her life once, and she would never forget it. Something as simple as an herb that grew locally in abundance had the power to fight the worst of Lily Brooke's demons.

She tip-toed away from the campfire scene and prayed to God that she would live to see another day.

Even though Magdalena knew her friends would be very upset with her for not waking them, she chose to go alone. She had caused them enough pain with the last adventure. Besides, she wasn't completely positive that it was werewolves she was hearing.

But just in case, better to go alone, she thought.

Gabriel must have sensed Magdalena's fear; he had a way of doing that, somehow, and woke up. He glanced around the campfire and realized nothing seemed amiss. He saw all his friends tucked into their sleeping bags, all cozy and warm.

Gabriel noticed the campfire was dwindling but still putting out ample warmth; no need to disturb anyone by adding more wood. He glanced at Magdalena's sleeping bag and saw her body tucked in tightly underneath the layers of blankets. He wondered why he had awakened but shrugged it off to the uncomfortable ground on which he was lying.

Thankful and taking in the moment, as the night was crystal clear with brightly shining stars,

Gabriel took notice of the well-lit woods and surrounding area. His gaze turned to the skies above, and he knew they had chosen the perfect night to go camping. The moon was full, and its light shined on the newly fallen snow, just perfectly. The glistening, snowy surface looked so much like diamonds sparkling in the night.

As Gabriel was admiring the beauty of it all, he happened to notice footsteps by Magdalena's sleeping bag. His heart skipped a little beat as he began staring at her, lying so still.

Then, a thought occurred to him. *Oh, no, maybe she isn't there after all!*

Gabriel slid out of his warm and comfortable sleeping bag and crawled over to where he thought Magdalena lie sleeping. Much to his surprise and chagrin, she wasn't there. What appeared to be her sleeping body, was wadded-up blankets she had used for warmth.

His mind went from calm to panic within seconds. Gabriel knew something was very wrong. He had awakened to something not right, but to what had him so perplexed. He stood there, wondering if he should awaken the others. This couldn't be good. Maybe, Magdalena had just heard something and wandered off; either way, he didn't like it, at all.

Before Gabriel could even think, Hubert woke up and saw him hovering in the light of the moon. Hubert panicked and screamed, waking up the rest of the group. Feeling a little irritated once he realized it was only Gabriel, Hubert was sure to speak his mind.

"What are you trying to do, Gabriel? Scare the beejezus out of everyone? I wake up in the dark, spooky woods in the middle of the night, and see someone standing over me, seriously. I told you that I would never be the same after we got chased by those demons," barked Hubert.

Gabriel knew everyone was now on edge, and he knew his news wasn't going to make anyone happier. But the longer he waited, the worse it could be for Magdalena if she were lost, or worse, in trouble. For all he knew, she was fine and out exploring. But, something about the situation had him feeling anxious.

"Sorry, Hubert. I didn't mean for everyone to wake up in a fright; but, I'm concerned," replied Gabriel.

With those words, everyone rose from their comfortable sleeping bags and began fully waking up. Greta realized that Magdalena seemed to be missing.

"Wait, where is Mags?" panicked Greta. "Where is she, Gabriel?"

Time seemed to stand still while everyone waited for Gabriel to respond.

"That's just it; I don't know. Something woke me up, and I'm not sure what. I noticed these shoe prints in the snow by the light of the full moon. They appear to be leaving Magdalena's sleeping bag, and she isn't here. I don't know what is going on, but we need to grab our flashlights and go find her."

"Oh, man, I knew this was a bad idea. I knew we didn't need to be out in these spooky woods at night. I knew better!" winced Hubert.

Everyone ignored Hubert's whining, as they were now all focused on figuring out where Magdalena had gone, and why she hadn't woken anyone up to go with her.

"Let's follow these tracks; everyone stays together. We have no idea what we may find," instructed Gabriel.

The five friends buttoned their coats, grabbed their flashlights, and followed Gabriel's lead. The shivering was something awful, and everyone knew it had nothing to do with the chilly air. All of their nerves were on edge, and it had something to do with the light of the full moon.

Gabriel led his friends through the woods, carefully following the footprints in the snow. Even though the light of the full moon tended to make everything feel a little spookier, it did lend enough light for them to be able to follow Magdalena's shoe prints on the newly fallen snow. They walked for what seemed like an eternity. But, about a mile into the woods, the footprints stopped in front of a dead tree.

"What? What does this mean? The footprints just ended; where is Magdalena? This makes no sense," wailed Piper. He had no intention of having any more of these super-duper scary experiences.

Gabriel stood frozen, as still as a statue. He looked all around him. He looked up into the tree, behind them, nothing made any sense at all. The footprints just ended. He didn't know what to do or what to say to the others.

"Hey, wait a second," said Cody. "Look closer, at Magdalena's shoe print."

Everyone got lower to the ground and followed Cody's gaze. There, beside the shoe print, were paw prints. Where the shoe print ended, the paw prints picked up.

Hubert couldn't hold it in any longer; he knew. He knew what had happened to Magdalena, and he blamed no one but himself.

Before anyone could speak, Hubert cried out, "It's all my fault! They have her! The werewolves have Magdalena, and I could have stopped it!"

Frozen in fear, everyone stood to stare at Hubert, just waiting for him to explain. But, all he did was stand there blubbering about how it was all his fault, and no one was getting any answers.

Gabriel crossed over to where Hubert was standing, placed his hands directly on Hubert's shoulders, looked him directly in the eye, and said, "Hubert, get ahold of yourself! What are you talking about? What has happened to Mags?"

"The book, the book, Gabriel, it's all in the book!" cried Hubert. His lips were trembling with fear, and he looked as white as a ghost.

With his patience dwindling very quickly, Gabriel asked again, "I don't have time to read the book, Hubert. What book, and what are you talking about? Where is Mags?"

Hubert realized his fear was taking over, and if he was right, and the werewolves had Magdalena, every second would count.

"The book we found in my basement, **Demonic Enchantments;** the book with the gold leaf on the cover. There is a chapter that talks about werewolves! I should have thought of it sooner! But, we were all so relieved that the demons were defeated and locked back up into the enchanted symbols, that it never occurred to me the werewolves would be hungry," cried Hubert.

The look of panic that swept across MALB's face was gruesome. As the realization dawned on them that something sinister, something as evil as werewolves, could have taken Magdalena hostage, it became direr than any of them could handle. At this very moment, the idea of Magdalena being captured by such evil creatures was worse than battling the demons face to face.

Gabriel felt sick. He thought he was honestly going to vomit.

The rest of the gang didn't look so good, either. Greta was sobbing with tears sliding down her cheeks while Piper and Cody were having another one of their complete body language conversations.

Not a word needed to be spoken; their expressions and body movements said it all.

Hubert, meanwhile, stood staring at his feet with tears rolling off his cheeks and onto the top of his boots.

Gabriel knew that he needed to take charge and fast.

"Okay, guys, it appears we missed a minor detail last fall when we thought we had everything buttoned up tightly. Let's think together. The demons are still locked up inside of the hidden lanterns, we know. But, we didn't realize their gatekeepers, the werewolves, would still be roaming the woods surrounding Lily Brooke. We can assume that Magdalena was either kidnapped from the campfire circle, or she heard them and decided to pursue on her own. It wouldn't be a surprise if only Magdalena could hear them, unlike us; think about it. She was the only one that could hear the mystic mumblings of the demons. She probably woke up hearing something in the woods and decided to investigate. Remind me to discuss this with her when we know she is okay," said Gabriel.

"I agree; but, why would her footprints end here, at this dead tree, and the paw prints pick up? Why here, and where did she go?" asked Greta.

"Great questions, and I honestly have no idea. I mean, on the other side of this tree is nothing but a steep slope dropping down the back of the mountain. There is no way she went down that slope; she wouldn't survive it," said Gabriel, as he stood looking out over the drop-off. There wouldn't even be anything to hold onto during the fall. No one would survive this treacherous terrain under these conditions.

But, the more Gabriel stood and thought about the scene before him, the more he knew Magdalena had gone down that slippery slope. She had to have gone down it. There was no place else that she could be. What made matters worse, he envisioned that whatever had been after her, or whatever she was following, had most likely also gone down the slippery slope. And, worse yet, the only way to save her was to go down the slippery slope.

At that moment, Gabriel knew the werewolves had chased her over the cliff. They were probably hiding in the dead tree, waiting on her to find them. They probably pushed Magdalena off the cliff!

Gabriel looked up to see all eyes on him. He knew that they knew. Everyone knew what must happen next. And, everyone knew what this meant. Would they ever see their beloved Magdalena again, alive? Even Hubert knew the next step in the game.

"So, I see by the look on everyone's face that you know Magdalena has gone down this slippery slope, and was most likely chased by the werewolves hiding in or behind this tree. And I also see that everyone understands this is the only way we will find her and be able to save her. I can't imagine a situation in which she doesn't need saving, just based on those monstrosities of paw prints," said Gabriel.

As he glanced around, by the light of the moon, he saw all heads shake in a 'yes' confirmation. It had been months since that abdominal pain had shot through his soul, but there it was, again — time to save his old pal and friend, Mags. Gabriel just prayed with everything inside of him that he would save her before the hungry werewolves planned dinner.

"Okay, so what is our plan?" asked Piper. "I mean, I know we are about to venture down that slope, and I know everyone here is going. But how exactly are we to do that?"

"Everyone, remove your jacket and tie the sleeves to another person's jacket sleeves. Let's make a train. It is our best chance of surviving the drop," suggested Cody.

"I like it!" exclaimed Gabriel. "Yes, everyone, tie your jacket sleeves together. The heavier the train is, the more ability we will have to steer instead of the steep slope controlling us."

With urgency, the five friends took off their coats and tied the sleeves together, making a long coat train. As they neared the edge of the slope, each one sat on their jacket and held on for dear life. This was about to be the ride of a lifetime.

Gabriel gave the go, and within seconds the train was off in flight. Before anyone could speak, the group was flying down the slippery slope, dodging trees, and hanging on with every ounce of strength they could muster. The ride seemed to last an eternity, and as they neared the bottom of the slope, they began to slow down, gradually. Coming to a full stop, everyone sat on their coats now wet with snow, with their hearts pounding out of their chests.

Grateful they had all survived, the friends began hugging each other and crying, as the emotions were so overwhelming. Step one was successful; they had survived the treacherous ride down the slippery slope. But, where was Magdalena?

Gabriel glanced around his surroundings, wondering where his best friend could be. Just a few feet away was the edge of a pond; the shimmer caught his eye. He jumped up and ran over to the edge of the pond. It seemed to be completely frozen, but he saw one of Magdalena's footprints by the edge. Oddly, there was only one shoe print and several paw prints right beside it, then, the edge of the frozen pond. That's it. But, this did confirm what he had thought; the werewolves had followed Magdalena over the cliff and down the slope.

Everyone had followed closely behind Gabriel, realizing he must have seen something. They saw the shoe print and the paw prints, and then nothing but a frozen pond.

"Um, any thoughts, guys?" asked Hubert. "I mean, Magdalena was here. And, there is nothing here now, but a frozen pond. Where is she?"

That seemed to be the million-dollar question. It appeared as though Magdalena had simply disappeared.

"There must be some explanation; she can't just disappear into thin air," responded Piper.

Hubert was doing his best to remember anything he could about the demonic book. *There must be some clue in that book*, he thought.

Before Hubert, or anyone else, had another thought, Gabriel noticed it. On the bank of the pond, off to the left a little away from where they stood, was a puddle. It had caught Gabriel's eye because it should have been frozen. The pond was frozen; as a matter of fact, everything was frozen. Why was that puddle not frozen? It struck him as being peculiar.

"Over there, guys! The puddle!" shouted Gabriel as he moved to get closer to the oddity.

"What about it?" asked Hubert. He found this a little ridiculous. It was simply a puddle of water. Demon werewolves were chasing Magdalena, and

Gabriel seemed focused on puddles of water, for goodness sake.

"Well, shouldn't it be frozen?" asked Greta. "Everything else is frozen! Including my hands!"

With that last comment from Greta, Hubert stood staring at the puddle.

Very interestingly weird, he thought. But, he no idea what it could mean. He was coming up with nothing.

Gabriel was obviously lost in thought as well, as he was now on his hands and knees peering into the puddle. He touched it, nothing happened. He stuck his hand into the puddle to find it was only about an inch deep. He sat back on his heels, contemplating the weirdness of it all, and then he saw it.

There was a paw print beside the puddle. As he sat there, Gabriel mused the werewolves were definitely chasing Magdalena. If the werewolves were near the puddle, so was Magdalena.

"Okay, guys. There is a paw print, here, beside the puddle. You know, this means Magdalena was here as well since we deduced the werewolves were chasing her. But, that I can tell, the paw prints end here. What does this mean?" asked Gabriel.

Each MALB member took their time getting down in the snow on their hands and knees, walking around the puddle and the surrounding area, looking for any clue. Well, everyone except for Hubert. He stood there, frozen stiff, wishing over and over in his mind for his fluffy pillow and soft comforter at home in his bedroom.

"Hubert!" snapped Greta. "Can you please help us figure this out? Believe me, we are ALL scared right now."

Embarrassed to be called out by a girl, Hubert began to walk around the puddle and look for clues while mumbling in his head. He was fairly certain this was as close to misery as anyone could get.

Hubert was so cold and irritable that he lost his balance and slipped right beside the puddle, destroying the paw print clue. Right about the moment that everyone started to yell at him, he disappeared completely into thin air. Gabriel, Piper, Cody, and Greta stood there, staring at the puddle in complete and utter shock.

Piper was the first to find his voice, and trembling, said, "Did Y'all just see that? I mean, did you see Hubert just completely disappear?"

"Um, yes, I saw it. But I don't know if I believe it. Could there have been something in that chocolate that Mrs. Mueller sent with Hubert for our smores that we had last night?" inquired Cody.

Gabriel had no words; none, at all. The only thing he could think of that made any sense, were these parts of the woods must not follow the same laws of nature as Lily Brooke; they must be enchanted. And, therefore, if he had learned anything from the adventure last autumn, in the world of enchantment, the laws of normal physics do not apply.

"So, apparently, these woods are overshadowed by enchantment and the laws of nature as we know them do not apply here. So, we need to stop thinking in terms of the reality we know and understand, and start thinking like Magdalena. As far as how or why Hubert just disappeared, yeah, you got me there," whispered Gabriel. He was feeling like such a failure, worried sick about his best friend, and standing there completely perplexed.

Greta cleared her throat, and everyone turned to face her.

"I have an idea. It sounds a little ridiculous, but work with me," said Greta. "Hubert slipped on the snow and ice, right here by the puddle. As he fell to the ground, he disappeared. What if he didn't disappear, but entered a secret passageway? You know, like in the sacrificial cave last fall?"

Gabriel instantly knew Greta was on to something.

"Yes! Greta! You are on to something, I can feel it. Remember when Magdalena stood between those boulders and the bright purple lights appeared, and the cave wall rose up like a garage door? Hubert must have triggered something that we can't see that somehow opened a secret passageway, similar to what happened in the cave a few months ago."

Piper and Cody were exchanging glances and not liking where this was going.

"I bet the secret passageway is hidden inside of that puddle," said Piper. "Think about it. We already realized something was odd about it because it isn't frozen like the pond. And, Hubert did fall right here."

"Well, maybe we should try to fall into the puddle. What do we have to lose at this point? We are already wet, cold, and miserable from the coat ride down the slope. Why not jump into a puddle?" smirked Greta.

"Okay, I will try first. If, for some reason, this works, everyone follow me! Lord only knows what we will find on the other side. Pray this works because if it doesn't, we are out of ideas," said Gabriel.

With that, Gabriel took a few steps backward, gave a little run, and slid towards the puddle just like he would slide into first base if he were playing baseball. He closed his eyes and almost prayed that he would enter the enchanted world that may lie behind the puddle. Not because he wanted another miserable and spooky adventure, but because the most important person in his life had gone through that secret entrance being followed by vicious and demonic werewolves. As Gabriel took one last breath before he hit the frozen ground, everything went black.

THE VORTEX

~ Four ~

Piper, Cody, and Greta stood there in anticipation as they watched Gabriel take the fall. Part of them wanted to see Gabriel disappear as they knew this would mean they could find Magdalena. Another part of them wanted to see Gabriel lying on the ground at their feet because if he did disappear, that meant they had to follow. And, jumping into anything that had the possibility of being enchanted, wasn't exactly exciting.

Before anyone could blink, Gabriel disappeared. There was no sign or trace of him anywhere.

The three children scrambled all around the puddle looking behind trees, looking in the frozen pond, looking everywhere they could think of because the alternative solution was more than they were prepared to embrace.

Realizing very quickly the choice had already been made for them, as there is no way they would leave their friends in such a terrible predicament, they began to huddle back around the puddle.

Meanwhile, Gabriel was trying to catch his breath while flying through endless, black space. He couldn't see anything; it was pitch black surrounding him. He felt the wind on his face as he was hurled through what appeared to be some type of vortex.

Gabriel felt his body flipping in circles, back and forth, and he absolutely had no control. The spiral motion of the descent into who knows what almost made him sick. Then, without notice, he landed flat onto his back.

The ground beneath him was hard and cold, yet smooth. As he lie there trying to gauge his surroundings, Gabriel realized he was in some type of a dark tunnel. His stomach began to churn as he realized he was underground.

Knowing time was of the essence, Cody, Greta, and Piper began to line themselves up to take the plunge into the puddle.

Piper stepped forward, knowing someone needed to and repeated Gabriel's actions.

Within a few seconds, poof, he was gone, too, nowhere to be seen. Left standing by the puddle, were the remaining two friends.

One by one, each took their turn and, with a leap of faith, jumped into the enchanted puddle of water. As they emerged from the vortex, landing on the ground, they all scrambled to their feet. Once they had their bearings, everyone stood looking at Gabriel with frightened eyeballs to eyeballs.

"Hey, guys, glad you decided to follow me. That was quite the trip, huh?" whispered Gabriel.

"Well, you can say that again!" mumbled Cody. "My back is killing me, and I'm fairly certain I won't be able to walk tomorrow. All those flips have me feeling a little woozy, too."

"Yeah, I know what you mean," responded Gabriel. "Well, at least now we know where Magdalena disappeared to after she slid down the slippery slope."

"Where are we?" asked Greta. "This looks like some type of tunnel. Are we underground?"

"That's what I am thinking. I am betting we are underneath the frozen pond," responded Gabriel.

"Oh, my gosh, this is too much for me, guys! I told you! I still have nightmares from the last expedition. I don't have any interest in chasing werewolves in the woods through a dang puddle that flips you around and lands you in some ridiculous underground tunnel beneath a frozen pond," retorted Hubert.

Everyone exchanged glances, not knowing whether to laugh at Hubert and his hysteria or cry because he did have a good point. But, realizing that

Magdalena was already down here alone with someone or something very evil in nature, was enough to get Gabriel back on task.

"Agreed! Let's find Magdalena and get the heck out of here!" exclaimed Gabriel.

But, before Gabriel could speak another word, much less come up with another plan, Hubert interrupted.

"And, exactly how are we going to get out of here once we find Mags? I mean, do you see a puddle that we can run and jump in for goodness sake? I mean, I hate to be the one to bring up bad news, but am I the only one feeling a little trapped right now?" panicked Hubert.

Greta could feel the sweat beginning to trickle down the side of her face. Hubert had a great point. The vortex they had just weathered, brought them from outdoors to the underground. There was no way they would be able to exit through the frozen lake. And, the entrance/exit to the vortex was hidden completely on this side.

The five children, feeling more like young children than teens, stood looking around, trying to find the exact spot in which they had emerged from the turbulent vortex. It appeared as though they had literally just fallen from nowhere. There was nothing but open space, darkness, and a dirt tunnel in which they were now standing.

"So, I don't have an answer to your question, Hubert, but I know if we don't get moving, Magdalena is getting further and further away from us. If we are stuck here, I would rather be stuck with a witch that has access to black magic than here alone with you," laughed Gabriel. He was praying his little attempt at humor would somehow take the edge off, at least.

No one laughed at Gabriel's joke but instead looked at him sympathetically. They knew he was coming unraveled, and apparently, it was beginning to show.

So, Gabriel took a deep breath and said, "Everyone, please, turn on your flashlight and let's get moving! Stay alert, and be sure to watch your surroundings as there is no telling where this tunnel will lead."

Everyone was thankful for the directions Gabriel had spoken as it gave them something to focus on, other than the dire circumstances they were now facing.

In a single-file line, with flashlights sweeping from side to side, the friends began walking through the dark and mysterious tunnel. Anticipation and anxiety were most definitely a force to be reckoned with the eminent sense of danger.

After what seemed like hours, the children finally exited the tunnel and found themselves standing outside in a forest. The sky was a beautiful midnight blue and was lit up with the most silver, sparkling stars they had ever seen. It was a beauty to witness, for sure.

The light of the stars was so vivid and provided such visual clarity that the landscape around them could be seen well.

Off into the distance, stood a magnificent castle. They had never seen anything so majestic and with such spectacular presence against the horizon. Well, maybe the monstrosity of the enchanted treehouse on MALB's last adventure, but this was even more intense and overwhelming than that.

"Do you guys see what I see?" asked Cody. "Do you see a huge, insane-looking castle off in the distance?"

"Um, yep," replied Hubert. "Great."

"Oh, boy, you can say that again," whispered Greta.

Meanwhile, Piper and Gabriel hadn't uttered a word. They were in awe. The picture that lie before them was like that of a fairytale. However, they were quick to remember that most fairytales ended happily ever after and didn't feature werewolves that were gatekeepers to demons. Nor, did they feature a storyline that had HUNGRY werewolves; great. Nor, did they feature a storyline with a thirteen-year-old witch being chased or kidnapped.

"So, I guess we have all figured out by now where we are going," said Gabriel. Even he couldn't hide the sense of looming dread in his voice.

"Looks that way," whispered Piper. "I think it would be better for us to turn our flashlights off, so they don't see us coming. The stars are shedding enough light that we should be okay to see without them."

"Good idea," agreed Gabriel.

Everyone turned off their flashlight and stored it in their coat pocket. No one seemed to notice how soaking wet their jackets still were from the sledding adventure earlier that night down the snowy slope.

All eyes were now focused on having to cross the open vastness of forest in order to get to the castle, preferably undetected. The unknown was bad enough without disturbing some wretched beast.

As Gabriel turned away from the castle, he saw the frozen pond. There it was, right behind them at the tunnel exit. He was having a tough time processing the fact that the vortex led from above ground to underneath the pond. And, somehow, the tunnel wove them from beneath the pond to here, somewhere in an enchanted forest; great. It just kept getting better and better.

Moving forward, the friends spread out while dodging behind trees, hiding behind bushes, and taking cover behind large rocks, every time they thought they heard a noise. It was almost as though someone or something was watching them closely. Gabriel knew it was most likely their nerves, but you could never be too careful.

As they neared the castle, it seemed to be too quiet. MALB huddled close together, and Gabriel whispered to the group, "This seems too easy, guys. It feels almost too quiet, almost as though they saw us coming and knew we would head straight for the castle. I'm beginning to feel a little sabotaged."

"Yeah, this doesn't feel very good to me, either," said Piper. "Maybe we should run back and hide in the woods; just watch the castle for a while."

Before anyone could respond, the howling screech was so loud it pierced their eardrums.

Everyone instinctively grabbed their ears and dropped to the ground in a duck and cover position.

The screech seemed to go on for several minutes. No one needed to speak. They all knew it was werewolves. And, they could all hear them.

They were in a new land, one that didn't identify with the physical laws they knew and understood. This was more of Magdalena's world, one with magic, one with unknown rules of its own. Gabriel had almost forgotten when they slid down the snowy slope that they had entered a new world. This one had a mind of its own. And, now, creatures of its own. They were about to battle the pure unknown.

"So, obviously, that was a werewolf or werewolves," said Greta. "We have to find Magdalena quickly!"

"But, we have nothing to protect ourselves. Flashlights won't scare werewolves!" cried Cody.

"Actually, they might!" shouted Hubert.

All eyes turned to Hubert. Everyone was silently praying he knew what he was talking about, this time.

"I remember reading about it in the book, **_Demonic Enchantments_**!" cried Hubert. "The reason they only come out at night, well besides being spookier that way, is they can't stand light!"

"You are a genius, Hubert!" cried Greta. She threw her arms around Hubert, and before he knew it, she planted a big sloppy kiss on his forehead.

"Yuck!" shouted Hubert as he quickly wiped the slobber off his forehead. "You can thank me later if that information helps us in some way. For now, let's all stay focused."

Inside, Gabriel was laughing. Hubert was all flustered now, and it showed. His face resembled the color of a bright red tomato.

"Alright, guys, let's make a plan," said Gabriel. "Keep your flashlights off as we decided earlier. Let's go ahead and enter the castle. If the werewolves are waiting on us, inside of the castle will be dark. If they don't like light, we won't run into any. So, once we sense they are near, or if we find Magdalena before, everyone, quickly turn on your flashlight and blind them."

All heads nodded in agreement. It wasn't much of a plan, but it was all they had.

So, again, they approached the castle as stealthily as they could. Along the way, they saw an old wooden sign announcing they had entered, *The Enchanted Forest*.

Great, the sign even announced the newly discovered forest was enchanted. Covered in moss, the sign appeared to be very old. Something about this entire place put everyone on edge.

As the friends neared the front of the drawbridge, everyone stopped. The ambiance of the moment didn't escape any of them. They all knew once they crossed that bridge, all bets were off, and each person would have to defend themselves to their greatest ability. They already knew there would be more than one werewolf to battle, as there were multiple paw print tracks back at the dead tree.

Taking a huge breath of air, the five MALB members grabbed hands for moral support and walked the length of the bridge. Each step seemed like an eternity. Each step brought them one step closer to evil. But each step also brought them closer to their best friend. And, right now, she needed them. So, right now, they would put their fears aside and move forward.

As they crossed over the threshold and entered the foyer area of the castle, the drawbridge slammed shut behind them.

Hubert jumped so high in fear that they thought he might fly out of the small window thirty feet above them.

It would have been funny if fear wasn't currently coursing through their veins. Everyone stood in complete darkness and understood they were not alone.

Evil was amongst them, and it was now time to play the game. It was pitch black in the castle foyer, which they all knew meant it was time to face the hidden beasts.

LINDTZL CASTLE

~ Five ~

While the five friends stood silently in the castle foyer wondering what to do next, Magdalena awoke to a large bump on the head. She tossed and turned, feeling sick to her stomach and quite dizzy.

As she slowly began to awaken, her mind started to panic as she began remembering the events from earlier that night. Magdalena remembered falling asleep in her warm, pink sleeping bag underneath the beautiful moonlit night, beside her best friends, and in the warmth of the glowing, amber campfire.

She remembered being awakened in the middle of the night by something. She hadn't been sure of what she heard, so she had paused in her sleeping bag, begging for sleep to return.

Then, it hit her. She remembered what she had heard, and the panic in the back of her throat was now funneling its way throughout her arms, legs, and torso. It was like a thousand tiny needle pricks all over her body.

Magdalena realized she had decided to venture out on her own, not wanting to risk any danger to her friends. She had tip-toed through the soft snow and into the dark woods near the coveted tire swing.

Finding herself deeper in the woods, she kept hearing the werewolves' cries off into the distance. She kept pushing through the dense forest, only to find herself at the end of a path, overlooking the bank of a steep cliff.

Magdalena remembered standing there and wondering where to go from here, as the path just ended at the base of an old, dead tree. She had leaned over the cliff to peer down and realized the drop-off led down a slippery looking slope with very treacherous terrain. She knew there was no way to get down the slope and survive it.

Then, she remembered turning back around to head back to the campfire but stood face to face with a three-headed werewolf.

She had read about werewolves in the book, **Demonic Enchantments**, the one that MALB had found hidden in Hubert's basement cellar, those fateful months prior. If it hadn't been for that book, they might have never solved the mystery of the crooked trail, for enchanted symbols and black magic was all new to Magdalena. But, luckily for the group, they hadn't encountered any werewolves in their last adventure, so the information hadn't seemed important. Well, it felt really important right about now.

Before Magdalena could react, the three-headed beast launched at her, throwing her over the cliff, and sent her flying through the air and down the slippery slope. She begged for her life and tried to wiggle free, but the werewolf had a firm grip on her coat. She could feel the drool sliding out of the creature's mouth onto the side of her face. The fear inside of her had been so encompassing.

Without warning, Magdalena and the three-headed monster landed violently on the snowy bank below, rolling head over heels for several moments, before finally coming to a complete stop.

That was the last memory she had of the ordeal. How she got into this dungeon looking of a room with a knot on her pounding head, was beyond her.

What to do now? She wondered.

Magdalena scanned the room, taking it all in at once. There was only one door, solid wood with a tiny arched window towards the top, which was covered with a black iron grate. Seeing the wrought iron made her instantly think of Gabriel and his dad, Otis Bach. The longing in her heart was almost more than she could bear as she realized it wouldn't be long before Gabriel and the others would awaken and realize she was missing.

Magdalena had no intention of disappearing, which she knew meant they would most definitely come looking for her. The guilt was agonizing as Magdalena lie there on the hard, cold, stone floor. Her body ached within every muscle and bone she possessed. The flight down the slope, fighting with the beast, and the harsh landing, left its mark.

While frantically trying to think of her next move, Magdalena wondered why she was still alive. Once they had landed at the bottom of the slope and she passed out, it would have been the perfect time for the werewolf to devour her.

Of course, she was thankful beyond measure that her life had been spared, but the purpose behind it was unknown. The only thing she knew for sure was that she needed to find a way out of this dungeon prison.

Magdalena pushed herself to sit up and sat there, patiently blinking, trying to let her vision adjust to the dimness of the room. She found herself shivering in the frigid air and noticed her coat and pants were wet from the snow. What she wouldn't give for her silky, pink pajamas and bedroom slippers back home in her room!

As her vision began to improve, Magdalena braced herself to stand. But, before she could get anywhere, she noticed movement in the far corner of the room.

Her heart began beating, and she knew that somehow, she was not alone. Scared to see who or what was in her dungeon cell, but knowing she had no option, she began to crawl on her hands and knees toward the corner where she had seen movement.

With pounding in her head, dread in her soul, and aching body, she inched closer, one tiny step at a time. Magdalena was virtually on top of the distant corner of the room when she saw it. She let out the most blood-curdling scream she could find from the depth of her gut.

There, in front of Magdalena's eyes, was a human skull and bones. The realization that someone had died in that very room, that someone had probably been just like her, in the wrong place at the wrong time, was more than she could handle.

Fear took over, and she couldn't think. Her mind was racing, and she noticed the rat hunched over in the deepest part of the corner. The movement she had seen must have been the rat as it scurried across the floor.

At a complete loss, Magdalena sat on her knees on the cold, hard floor, rocking back and forth with her arms hugging herself, silently crying. Her future seemed very bleak. The werewolf must have spared her for this horrific punishment.

Would she ever see the other side of that dungeon room door? She wondered. *Would she ever see her best friends again?*

As the rest of MALB stood frozen in the dark, mysterious castle foyer, they heard the scream. Every single one of them knew it was Magdalena. On the one hand, they were grateful she was still alive, and they had confirmation she was here with them. On the other hand, her scream was real. They knew that whatever had happened to her must be terrible.

"Oh, my gosh, that is Magdalena!" cried Greta. "Hurry, we have to do something! Gabriel, what do we do?"

Gabriel stood, his heart pounding in his chest, in the dark foyer. He knew one wrong step could be death for all of them. And, that most definitely would not help Magdalena. His mind raced as he stood there, contemplating the next move.

Before he could respond, Hubert exclaimed, "We are all goners! We are all going to die!"

"Hubert, stop it! We can't give up because we are scared. We must push through the fear and think logically," demanded Gabriel.

"Okay, man, I'm all ears. What do we do?" exclaimed Hubert.

Gabriel knew he was quickly running out of time. No matter what he decided to do, it had to be now.

"Could anyone tell which direction Magdalena's scream came from?" asked Gabriel.

"I'm not sure, but it almost seemed like it came from underneath us," replied Cody.

"Yeah, it sounded muffled like it was from somewhere below us," agreed Piper.

"Okay, we need to find a staircase or an elevator, something that will get us below this floor," said Gabriel.

"Well, dude, it's dark. What do you suggest?" whined Hubert. "I'm not about to die in a dang haunted castle where werewolves live!"

"To be honest with you, Hubert, no one plans on dying today. But you have a good point. I can't see a thing. I can't even see you standing near me," retorted Greta.

"Alright, everyone, keep your nerves in check. We have been in scary situations before and survived just fine. But, we must stay focused and work together," muttered Gabriel.

"I have an idea. Let's use only one flashlight. It will give us enough light to see where we are going without alerting anyone we are here," suggested Piper.

"I like it," said Gabriel. "Everyone, let's use my flashlight."

With that, Gabriel pulled his flashlight out of his coat pocket and turned it on. The small amount of light was almost blinding to all five of them as their eyes weren't accustomed to any light, whatsoever. It took a few moments, but slowly they all began to see each other standing in the dark castle entryway.

"Man, I am so glad only to see the five of us standing here and not some werewolves!" exclaimed Hubert.

Everyone had to give a little chuckle at Hubert's words. He always seemed to find a way to break the ice, so to speak. And right now, they could all use a little comedic relief.

Gabriel swept the area of the entryway with the flashlight and confirmed they were all alone. The drawbridge must be programmed to close every time someone crosses over the threshold. At least they weren't standing face to face with some demonic beast at the moment.

"Everyone slowly branch out a little and feel the walls to see if you can find a way out of this foyer. We need to find anything that appears as though it will help us get further into the depths of the castle," instructed Gabriel.

The friends began frantically looking for any hidden lever, staircase, trap door, or elevator. They knew time was ticking and who knew what was happening to Magdalena.

After about a solid five minutes, in defeat, Cody said, "This is an entryway to a castle. How can it not have any hallways, doors, stairs, anything? There is no way we are standing in a space with no exit."

Gabriel wanted to pull his hair out. Then, it occurred to him.

"Guys, we are going about this all wrong! We forget the most important aspect of all."

"What? I'm all ears," smirked Greta. She was tired, cold, wet, hungry, and exhausted.

"The Enchanted Forest is just that, enchanted. This castle doesn't play by our rules. It has its own set of laws. I am betting it is made to look as though there is no passageway in case pure humans ever happened upon the castle. We need to think as Magdalena would think," whispered Gabriel.

"You're right!" said Piper. "But, does anyone have any ideas?"

Hubert felt this uneasy queasiness in his gut. He wasn't sure where it was coming from, or quite frankly what it meant, but he knew something was right at his fingertips.

"Light. Whatever we are supposed to do, it has something to do with light. I don't know why, but I can just feel it. Maybe we should shine the flashlight intensely on one section of the wall or something, instead of scanning the room with it. Maybe the light will somehow activate a wall," suggested Hubert.

Gabriel stood there almost stunned that Hubert would have such an intellectual idea. Typically, Hubert was the scared one that would reluctantly follow the group, simply because he didn't want to be the one left out. But, here he was, recommending an idea that would potentially bring them face to face with evil.

Hubert sensed the silence in the room and responded to what he knew was running through everyone's mind.

"Yes, I know you are all wondering why I said this. And, I know that you know, well, we all know that there is no way that I want to venture into this castle any further than where I am currently standing. But, Magdalena is our friend, and somehow that dang book has changed my thoughts. So, if I can't go home and go to bed, let's go save our friend."

Hubert's words were the fuel the team needed.

Gabriel took his flashlight and began aiming it at each wall, a few minutes at a time; nothing happened. Everyone stood there, wondering what to do next. Then, he had an idea. Gabriel walked over to the drawbridge wall, the door they had walked through when entering the castle. Thirty feet above him was the tiny window. Just beneath the little window was a wooden plank hung on the stone wall.

The words 'Lindtzl Castle' was carved into the plank. Gabriel aimed the flashlight on the drawbridge door as intensely as he could; nothing happened.

"Lindtzl Castle," said Cody. "Really makes you wonder who Lindtzl is and what happened to him or her."

"Not really!" responded Hubert. "I don't want to know!"

Before anyone could wager or guess as to where the name Lindtzl came from, Greta's voice rang in their ears.

"Wait, Gabriel! You may be on to something!" exclaimed Greta. "Everyone, take your flashlights, and let's all aim them at the door together!"

Everyone scrambled to get their flashlights out of their coat pockets. Within a moment or two, all five flashlights lit up the drawbridge door. The light was so bright that it was almost blinding. In seconds, the ground beneath MALB began to rumble and move. Whatever they were doing, it must be working!

As the ground was shaking, Gabriel realized the stones were moving. The ground movement came to a stop, and everyone followed Gabriel's lead by shining the light on the floor.

There, in front of their eyes, was a hidden staircase that seemed to go to the depths of the earth. The friends exchanged frightened glances as they each realized the next move was to descend the dark steps.

"Oh, man! This is NOT what I had in mind!" shouted Hubert. He was almost wailing at this point.

"Hubert, without you, we would have never thought to use light. You are a hero!" gasped Gabriel.

Hubert loved attention, and everyone knew it. But, this wasn't the kind of attention he found himself wanting, right now. But, he did like Magdalena and wanted to save his friend, so he fully accepted the plight he currently found himself facing.

"Aw, gee, guys. Thanks! But, all we have now is another mystery and some demonic, scary, dark castle steps," Hubert sheepishly responded.

"Well, five minutes ago, we had nothing," answered Cody. "So, let's go, guys. We all know which direction we are headed."

"Alright, let's go back to using only one flashlight. The last thing we need is to alert our captors and, worse, run out of flashlight batteries," said Gabriel. "I will go first and lead the way."

Knowing that Hubert always wanted to be the last in line as he thought that would allow him to be the first to run in any scary situation, Gabriel suggested, "Hubert, why don't you take up the back of the line and alert us of anything coming from behind?"

Hubert thought that was the best idea he had heard all day! Secretly, he called this philosophy his sanity insurance. He would be the first one to escape if any demons, werewolves, or whatever the haunt of today came his way.

"Sure! I got y'all covered here from the back," responded Hubert, with a sly smile that no one could see in the dark.

One by one, the five friends descended the dark, stone steps leading underneath the castle to who knows what, by the light of one flashlight. Gabriel prayed with everything inside of his soul that he would find his beloved Magdalena safe and sound, somewhere in the bowels of the castle.

The spiral staircase wound around and around and around, to the point everyone was beginning to feel very dizzy. It took about ten minutes for the group to finally reach the bottom of the eerie staircase.

"Well, one thing is for sure; if we need to get out of here in a hurry, it won't happen," said Cody. "We just spent ten minutes going down these stairs."

Gabriel knew Cody was right, so he didn't utter a word. He thought it best to move forward and not dwell on their dire circumstances.

Magdalena sat in her dungeon cell, wondering what was happening. Suddenly, the room began to shake violently. It felt like an earthquake, and then just as quickly, it stopped.

She sat, still crunched over on her knees sobbing, trying to listen for any detection of noise outside of her stone walls. Her sixth sense must have been activated because she felt a presence. Somehow, she knew her friends were coming to save her. Maybe her plight wasn't as desperate as it seemed. She stood up, crossed over to the door, and began screaming help as loudly as she could.

Before MALB could take another step, while standing there wondering what to do now, Piper said, "Shh! I think I hear someone or something! It is coming from that direction!" as he pointed to the right.

Gabriel shined his flashlight to the right, and they soon realized that where they stood at the bottom of the spiral staircase was a huge fork that led in four different directions. Piper had pointed to the far-right path. As Gabriel stood at the entrance to the path, everyone remained as quiet as they could, trying to hear any noise.

"I hear it!" exclaimed Gabriel. "It must be Magdalena! It almost sounds like, help!"

With that, the five friends began moving as fast as they possibly could down the dark and windy path, following the sound. They silently prayed they would find their friend unharmed, and soon.

After what seemed like an eternity, the path ended at a wooden door with a tiny wrought iron opening. As they arrived at the door, they could hear Magdalena's unmistakable voice on the other side, yelling for help.

"Magdalena! We're here! Is that you?" shouted Gabriel.

"Yes! Oh, my goodness, yes! Help me, please! There is a dead body in here, and a rat!" cried Magdalena.

Any other time, Cody and Piper would have snickered at the idea of Magdalena being scared of a rat. She was a witch for goodness sake. Something about a witch being scared of a rat was quite humorous.

However, the thought of a dead body being on the other side of that door tended to take the humor right out of the situation.

In the dim light cast by Gabriel's flashlight, the mood wasn't lost on any of them as their faces looked identical. The look of fear tends to be one of those basic human reactions that everyone possesses.

As they all stood there looking at each other and allowing Magdalena's words to sink in, the dread in the room magnified. They had to find a way through that solid wood and wrought iron door to get to their best friend, and unfortunately, a dead body. Great.

SPOOKY SKELETONS

~ Six ~

Magdalena stood frantically at the door. Her prayers had been answered! She knew her friends wouldn't let her die in that horrible, stone-cold dungeon room, all alone. She began pounding on the door, crying out to each one of them in yelps of thank you. Her fear had completely seized her every being.

"Mags, calm down!" shouted Gabriel. He knew she needed to remain calm because, at this point, they hadn't figured out how to get through the door.

"I'm trying! But hurry! Get me out of here!" screeched Magdalena.

"We are Mags! We won't leave here without you, but you need to remain calm and think. We have to get through this door!" responded Gabriel.

Magdalena stood, staring at the ironclad door. She knew there would be no way to get through that door. And, she had the proof in a pile of bones, right beside her. Her mind refused to accept anything less than getting out of that castle and back home. But, how to make it all happen was something she hadn't quite figured out.

"Magdalena, do you know where you are?" asked Cody. He wanted to get a sense of how injured she may be, knowing she had fallen down the slippery slope.

"No! I fell off a cliff, was chased by a three-headed werewolf, and woke up in this dungeon room with a huge lump on my head. Where am I?" cried Magdalena.

The rest of MALB, on the other side of the door, stood frozen in fear.

"Did you say a three-headed werewolf? Not like, three separate werewolves?" whispered Greta.

"Yes! It was one werewolf with three heads!" answered Magdalena. "I've never seen anything so hideous in my life!"

"Oh, my God; I'm done; toast. I am toast now, guys. I can't do this; nope; not me," demanded Hubert.

The lump in the back of Gabriel's throat must have been the size of a small boulder, as he couldn't swallow, no matter how hard he tried. The realization of how wicked and enchanted this place must really be was almost more than even he could comprehend. And, he still had Magdalena on one side of the door and the rest of MALB on the other side of the door.

"Mags, I need you to listen to me and focus. This is very important," said Gabriel.

"Okay, Gabriel. I am listening. What do you have in mind?" answered Magdalena.

"When you fell over the cliff with the werewolf chasing you, I am assuming, you must have landed near a frozen pond," stated Gabriel.

"Yes, I remember falling down the cliff with the three-headed monster attached to me and tumbling on the snow at the bottom. I remember we wrestled a little on the landing, and I saw a pond right beside where we stopped rolling. That is the last thing I remember as I must have blacked out," informed Magdalena.

"Okay, this is good. At least you remember that much. The pond you saw was frozen. Right beside the pond was a puddle of water. It struck us as being odd because it wasn't frozen like the pond. Hubert slipped and fell into the puddle and disappeared into thin air," explained Gabriel.

"Um, what did you say, Gabriel?" responded Magdalena.

"Yes, I know this is a lot to take in at once. Stay with me. Once Hubert disappeared into the puddle, the rest of us followed him. We entered some type of vortex. It was very turbulent, dark, and seemed to go on forever. We landed on a dirt floor, and once we got our bearings, we realized we were in an underground tunnel. The vortex we entered through the puddle took us beneath that frozen pond. As we followed the dirt tunnel, it led to a sign," said Gabriel.

"Do I want to know what the sign said?" inquired Magdalena. She was desperately trying to make any sense of what Gabriel was saying. Puddles, frozen ponds, and a vortex?

"Oh, I assure you, you DON'T want to know!" shouted Hubert.

The rest of MALB gave Hubert a dirty look, the kind that said hush!

Gabriel continued, bracing for impact. "The sign said, 'The Enchanted Forest.'" whispered Gabriel.

Magdalena stood there a few moments letting her mind process Gabriel's words. Here she was again, being chased by demonic creatures, and landing somehow in an enchanted forest.

Could this day possibly get any worse? She wondered.

"So, we have ourselves another unwanted adventure, I see," mumbled Magdalena. "Where are we right now?"

"Well, once you enter the forest and see the sign, off in the distance there is a majestic looking castle. We are currently in the basement of that castle. And I might mention, so far it appears deserted which we know isn't true," answered Gabriel. "Otherwise, you wouldn't be locked up in that room."

Magdalena couldn't believe it. Here they were, again! The first time she had decided to leave the safety of her own home to meet her childhood friends for one evening together, they find themselves in a desperate mystery again.

This really wasn't fair, she thought.

"I have experienced just about every emotion possible tonight. I am exhausted, wet, hungry, weak, and scared to death. But, if it is the last thing I do, I will not let that beast get the best of me!" shouted Magdalena.

There she was, thought Gabriel.

There was his beloved Mags. She was gaining strength, which he knew was the only way this mystery would be solved, letting them all get back home safely.

"Hey, Mags, I don't know if it matters at all, but we saw the words 'Lindtzl Castle' engraved above the drawbridge door in the foyer," said Cody.

Magdalena's thoughts were racing, as she was frantically trying to think if the name Lindtzl was familiar. She was coming up with absolutely nothing.

"That name doesn't sound familiar to me," whispered Magdalena. "I don't know if it has any relevance at all, but good to know. So, how did you find me here in the dungeon cellar?"

"Actually, it was Hubert that had a breakthrough," replied Gabriel.

Hubert's face turned red; he could feel it. Luckily though, in the dark basement, no one could see it.

Gabriel continued, "He remembered reading about the werewolves in the golden leaf book and realized they hate light. When we entered the castle, everything was dark, no light to be found. Once we realized the forest and everything in it doesn't operate by rules of our world, only rules of enchantment, we knew it would take something significant to find an opening. Hubert realized that since werewolves live in the castle, or at least have access to it, they probably hate light. So, we took the flashlights and shined them on the walls hoping to find secret access."

Greta noticed Gabriel seemed to be getting tired, so she continued. "Nothing was happening, so we decided to use all of our flashlights and shine them on the drawbridge door which had closed once we entered the castle, leaving us trapped. Once the intensity of the light was concentrated on that one wall, a hidden stone staircase opened in the foyer floor. We followed this spiral staircase for about ten minutes, which ended at a fork leading to four different tunnel paths. That's when we heard you screaming for help, and we took the path to the far right, trying to find you. It led us directly to this door."

Magdalena was taking it all in, and without realizing it was back in sleuth mode. She was wondering the significance of the four separate tunnel paths.

In their last adventure, there had been a fork in a path which led to two completely different trails. One had been crooked, and one had been straight and narrow.

The crooked trail had led them to the sacrificial cave, where the golden leaf had been found, ultimately saving MALB from the demons. She couldn't help but wonder if there was any significance to the separate paths underneath Lindtzl Castle. Or, it could be that each path led to a different dungeon.

"So, I am wondering if there is any significance between the four separate basement tunnel paths. I may just be making something out of nothing, but the last fork in the path we happened upon a few months ago led to very different outcomes. I can't help but wonder if each one of those tunnel paths leads to a different dungeon, or if they represent something much worse," suggested Magdalena.

Poor Hubert, he had enough of this stuff. He just wasn't built for this kind of stress, and he knew it.

"Guys, I don't care where each of the four tunnel paths leads. Can we rescue Magdalena somehow, and go home? We don't need to try and discover everything that Lindtzl Castle may offer," whined Hubert.

Greta couldn't help but silently agree with Hubert. She seriously just wanted to get Magdalena out of that dungeon and get the heck back home. Sometimes solving mysteries just wasn't what it was cut out to be. They were much more fun when they were made-up mysteries during their young childhood days. Now, the intensity of the situation seemed to be unraveling all of them.

Gabriel knew everyone wanted the same thing, except for Magdalena, maybe, and he knew that the best way to keep everyone engaged was to keep moving forward. The longer they stood there contemplating the dire situation, the worse it would become.

"Mags, you may be on to something. But for now, let's figure out how to get you out of there!" exclaimed Gabriel.

Magdalena stood lost in thought and said, "I have an idea. Let's go with what we know works. The light from the flashlight opened a hidden staircase before, let's try it again. Maybe, just maybe, it will open this door!"

"Great idea, Mags!" shouted Piper. This was an idea he welcomed almost as much as Thanksgiving feast.

Everyone grabbed their flashlight and began aiming it at the solid dungeon door. Gabriel was hoping with everything inside of him that this would work because if it didn't, he was out of ideas.

After about two or three minutes of all five flashlights concentrating on the dungeon room door handle, the door opened.

Gabriel stood, staring at the opened door. It really couldn't be that simple. He knew there would be some type of price of pay. It couldn't be this simple.

"No one moves!" shouted Gabriel.

Everyone stood frozen in their tracks, Magdalena included.

"What is wrong with you, Gabriel?" shouted Hubert. "The door is open!"

"Precisely," responded Gabriel. "It is too easy. It has got to be a trap. Yes, light unlocked the door but without any resistance. It can't be!"

Magdalena quickly picked up on Gabriel's line of thinking. Wondering how to test the doorway, she stood lost in thought.

"So, no one is going to like this idea, especially Magdalena, but I think I know how we can test the door access without finding ourselves eaten alive by a werewolf," said Piper.

All eyes turned to him.

"Go on," said Hubert.

"If we throw the dead body in Magdalena's room through the doorway, the movement will be sensed, and we can see what happens," explained Piper.

"Oh, that is a great idea," responded Gabriel. "Mags, I know you don't like it, but I would rather something happen to the poor soul in your dungeon room than you!"

"Well, to be honest, there isn't a dead body here in my dungeon room," said Magdalena.

Everyone looked at each other, wondering why Magdalena would have made up such a horrible thing.

"Let me explain; I know what everyone is thinking," said Magdalena. "What is in my room are remains of a body, a human skeleton!"

Hubert felt like he was going to faint. Realizing how long someone must have been trapped in that dungeon room for there to be a skeleton inside, made him go weak in the knees.

If fear had a name, it was Lindtzl Castle. Whatever had happened here, and whoever had died in that room, was now about to be bait for a potential booby trap in the doorway.

Before anyone could speak, Magdalena walked over to the skeleton, picked it up, and threw it through the open dungeon door. About the time the bones crossed the threshold, the floor opened from beneath, and the skeleton went crashing below.

Everyone stared in amazement at the exposed dungeon room beneath the dungeon in which they were still standing. But, what they saw in that room was nauseating.

As the six MALB members stood gazing at the open ground in front of them, they saw piles of skeleton bones. The stack of bones must have been eight feet high. There had been many deaths in this castle. The hair on all their arms was standing straight up, and their tongues were frozen in fear. No one in that room lost sight of the fact that if Magdalena had run through the door when it opened, she would now be on top of the wall of spooky skeletons.

Magdalena broke out in a cry of pain, realizing how Gabriel had just saved her life when he had screamed for no one to move. Her mind was spinning, her pulse was wickedly fast, and she felt like she was going to faint.

"How do I get out of here?" winced Magdalena.

"Okay, I think the booby trap has presented itself, so now you should be clear to jump over the opening," replied Piper.

"You want me to JUMP over that pit of bones?" cried Magdalena. "What if I miss?"

"We've got you, Mags. Let's go; do this so we can get out of here!" demanded Hubert.

Magdalena knew there was no other way she was getting out of that dungeon, so without another thought, she took a running leap and jumped for dear life. She landed on the other side of the skeleton pit, literally on top of Hubert.

"Well, Hubert, you did want her to jump," laughed Greta.

It was a comedic moment that everyone in that basement dungeon needed. It was almost like oxygen to the brain.

Everyone hugged each other, and tears of joy were found on each face in that dark, dungeon tunnel. They had saved their friend, and now the task was to get back home.

"Thank goodness! Now, let's get out of here before the werewolves figure out we have Magdalena," whispered Cody.

The friends quickly scrambled to their feet and retraced their steps back to the fork at the bottom of the stone staircase. But, before they could take one step, the sound of panting dogs was coming from above. Instantly, they knew their whereabouts had been discovered. Left with no other option, they realized they would have to choose one of the other three tunnel paths to hide.

Gabriel looked at Magdalena, Cody looked at Piper, and Greta glanced at Hubert. All six of them knew this was a matter of life and death. Should they pick tunnel number two, three, or four? Tunnel number one had led them to a bunch of skeletons, as well as Magdalena. But this time, escape was the name of the game. Which would it be?

TUNNEL NUMBER THREE

~ Seven ~

It was the luck of the draw. The friends began running down tunnel number three. Number one was off to the right, where they had found Magdalena. Tunnel number two was right in front of the stone steps, so they figured the werewolves would search that tunnel first after they discovered Magdalena had escaped. Tunnel number four put them further away from the stone staircase leading to the castle foyer, so they opted for tunnel number three.

Ultimately, Gabriel was fairly certain that all these underground dungeon tunnels probably led to something very unpleasant. But, at the moment, a three-headed hungry and upset werewolf didn't sound like a viable option, either.

With only Gabriel's flashlight on, the six children moved as quickly as they could in the unfamiliar surroundings. Secretly, they were all praying that somehow, they would find a way out of the enchanted castle before the werewolves learned of their exact whereabouts.

As they neared the end of the tunnel, they stood facing a fireplace. MALB turned to each other in a complete stupor.

"Oh, no, why would there be nothing but a fireplace at the end of a dungeon tunnel?" asked Greta.

"You have got to be kidding me!" shouted Hubert. "Are we ever going to get out of here?"

Hubert's words rang true for everyone's sentiments. This castle held more mysterious and puzzling scenarios than anyone could dream up.

Gabriel approached the fireplace, trying to see if he could find any type of a lever, handle, or anything at all.

"Everyone, watch your footing. I'm looking for a lever, handle, something that will open the floor or move a wall. We know what happened with the skeleton pit, so be sure if the floor moves to jump quickly!" warned Gabriel.

Everyone began staring at the floor, not paying any attention to what Gabriel was doing as no one wanted to fall into a pit of old bones.

Gabriel found nothing around the fireplace, so the six of them stood looking at each other.

"Wait, I have an idea," said Magdalena.

She walked up to the fireplace and put her hands inside of it. There was no fire or wood, but just a fireplace. She thought to herself that it seemed staged. And, the only way to test it was to put her hands inside of it while praying nothing pulled her inside.

As Magdalena pulled her hands back out of the fireplace, the wall rotated, just like the one they had discovered at their church, St. Irmgardis! The rotating wall had been found in a closet of the church and had led to the hidden dungeon where the *chosen ones* of Lily Brooke secretly met.

Magdalena felt the chills run up and down her spine, as she hadn't thought about that rotating wall or dungeon since she and Gabriel had hidden on top of that elevator, eavesdropping on the secret society's emergency meeting.

Hubert's words brought Magdalena back to the present moment.

"Wow! Look at that!" shouted Hubert.

All eyes were now facing a room with a large conference table, twelve chairs, walls of bookshelves, and a real fireplace against the farthest wall from the entryway.

The friends walked forward into the hidden room they had discovered behind the faux fireplace wall.

"This is a hidden meeting room, I'm thinking," said Gabriel. "Maybe, it was created for emergencies since it is tucked down here in the castle dungeon."

Cody and Piper were in awe of the hidden room. It was so cozy. The table and twelve chairs were made from solid mahogany wood. The detail and design work on the table and chair legs were top notch.

As they all walked the perimeter of the room, they realized the books stored on the wall bookshelves were quite exquisite. Beside the real fireplace found on the far wall of the room was a stack of cut wood and a box of matches.

"Okay, guys, this is the perfect place for us to hide. Let's close that hidden rotating wall so the werewolves can't find us. Then, we can gather our thoughts on what to do next. Maybe, some of these books will help us figure out our next move," suggested Gabriel.

"But, if we close the rotating faux fireplace wall, what if we can't get back out?" asked Greta.

Cody gave her words some thought and replied, "Yes, good point. However, if the werewolves enter this tunnel and we leave the wall open, and they see us, there is nowhere for us to go. We will die in this dungeon tunnel; it is our only chance."

Knowing Cody was right, Greta nodded her head in agreement.

Gabriel addressed the group. "So, we are all in agreement to close the rotating wall?"

As Gabriel glanced around the room, he got five affirmative head nods. So, he walked over to the wall and quietly closed it.

"I sure hope this room is soundproof," mumbled Hubert.

Once the wall was closed, everyone seemed to relax just a little. It had already been quite the night, and everyone knew from prior experience the evening was just beginning. What started as a friendly camping excursion amongst life-long childhood friends, had quickly turned unfortunate, to put it mildly.

Hubert and Greta grabbed a seat at the long conference table. The weariness was beginning to show on each of their faces. Sledding down a steep, treacherous slope, falling through a black vortex, and hiding from demonic werewolves had already tapped their energy potential for one night. And, the end was nowhere in sight.

The rest of MALB began browsing the books located on the shelves around the room. Maybe, somehow, they would find a book that gave them more information about the predicament they currently found themselves entangled. The room was filled with silence, and there wasn't a child in the room that wasn't thankful for a few moments of peace.

Hubert was still soaking wet from the evening's travels, so he casually walked over to the fireplace to start a fire. He knew everyone in the room was sporting wet clothing, and the air temperature in the dungeon tunnel was quite chilly. Before long, the fire was roaring, and the warmth could be felt around the room.

"Oh, Hubert, thank you so much for building that fire," exclaimed Magdalena. Her head was still pounding, but she didn't dare mention it to her friends. They had risked their lives that night trying to save her, and the last thing she was going to do was complain. Why, if it weren't for the gang, she would have died in the lonely dungeon cell room, and there were skeleton bones to prove it!

"You're welcome, Mags. I figure we could all use a little warmth and rest," replied Hubert. He walked back over to the conference room table and took his seat. Before he knew it, his head was lying on his folded arms propped up on the long table, and his eyes were closed.

No one woke Hubert up from his slumber, as they figured he needed the rest. His stress level had seemed extremely high, although very warranted, and the rest of MALB knew it was best to let him doze.

Greta sat at the table, wondering how the night would end. She didn't dare voice her concerns as that wouldn't help anyone in the room, but she didn't see a way out of their current circumstances, at all.

Here they were, trapped in the basement of a huge castle found in an enchanted forest, and the only exit was being guarded by werewolves that were loyal to the very demons they had recently defeated. And MALB had thought the last adventure was difficult, but this one seemed virtually impossible.

"Oh, this may be useful!" exclaimed Magdalena.

She turned around to face everyone in the room and said, "The title of this book is '**The History of Queen Lindtzl.**'"

"Yes, that certainly seems interesting," replied Cody.

"I'll say," replied Gabriel. "Maybe, it will give us some clues as to what has happened here. I mean, the place seems deserted except for the werewolves, and who knows what else that goes spook in the night."

"I'll check it out; the rest of you keep looking for more clues," stated Magdalena.

Magdalena took a seat at the long conference table, beginning to feel sleepy as the warmth of the fire was quickly making the room much cozier. But, she knew that she needed to maintain her focus and find some answers before they become someone, or something's, dinner. She took a deep breath, opened the book, and prayed to find something of substance between the old, worn, yellow pages.

Cody, Piper, and Gabriel stayed focused on the books that lined the walls from floor to ceiling. Greta sat transfixed on her hands, and Hubert was softly sleeping at the table.

"Wait! Here is a book on werewolves!" shouted Piper. "Maybe, we can see what makes these creatures tick!"

"Fantastic!" responded Gabriel. "Go check it out; I'm going to keep scanning these walls."

Piper joined Magdalena at the table and began researching all he could find about werewolves.

The silence in the room was deafening, and it wasn't lost on any of them that their future may come down to the words written in a book from long ago. Realizing the plight which they now faced, it did have a sense of irony.

As everyone sat focused on their respective duties, they heard movement coming down tunnel number three. Magdalena gently woke Hubert and gave him the shh! symbol with her finger pressed lightly to her lips. He understood and sat frozen in his seat. All heads were scanning the room, and everyone was looking at each other while silently praying the werewolves wouldn't detect the heat coming from the hidden conference room fireplace.

As the werewolves reached the rotating wall, you could hear their growls from inside of the hidden room. They detected something was amiss, but luckily for MALB, the werewolves must not have put too much thought into it. After a few minutes, they seemed to turn around and leave tunnel number three. Waiting for an additional ten minutes or so before anyone spoke, MALB stood like mannequins just praying they weren't detected.

Finally, Gabriel spoke, "I think we are okay now. They most definitely sensed we had been in tunnel number three at the faux fireplace wall. We all heard the growls, but they must not know about the hidden rotating wall or this conference room. Thank goodness for that small miracle tonight. We could sure use another one, though, as I can't seem to come up with any plan that will get us out of this dungeon room alive."

"Well, I may have an idea," said Magdalena.

All eyes turned to hear what Magdalena had to say. If anyone could save them, it would be her!

"Well, this castle was built years ago for Queen Lindtzl. Her husband, Charles Lindtzl, the King, was attacked one night while wandering The Enchanted Forest. They never determined what exactly happened, as his guards were left unscathed with mysterious memory loss, but they believe his horse and cart were sabotaged by werewolves that belonged to the demons that lived here in the forest."

"Woah, that is just plain creepy! I sure hope they aren't the same werewolves chasing us!" cried Hubert.

"You can say that again," whispered Greta.

"History has it that King Lindtzl was a *chosen one*. In other words, he was a wizard. Now, that isn't too surprising since this forest is enchanted. You would think the demons, werewolves, and Lindtzl kingdom lived in some type of harmony since everything here was affected by enchantment, in some capacity. But, legend says the werewolves killed King Lindtzl."

"Why do I have a feeling that is the reason they were calling out to you tonight, Magdalena? I mean, you are a *chosen one,* and you were the only one to wake up tonight when they were howling. But, what do they want with you, now?" asked Cody.

"Good point, Cody," replied Magdalena. "I definitely agree with you on why they are targeting me. But there has to be a bigger reason than simply, I'm a *chosen one*."

Magdalena sat a little confused.

Why now? She thought.

"Well, actually, think about it. You defeated the three demons, including the grand demon, a few months ago, and locked them up for eternity in the enchanted symbols, the lanterns. The werewolves that are after us were the gatekeepers for those three demon heads; this must be retribution. Something must have happened after King Lindtzl was killed, and the werewolves must have somehow overtaken this castle. We just witnessed that they weren't familiar with this hidden room," suggested Gabriel.

Magdalena could feel the steam coming out of her ears.

"Yes! That's it! It makes perfect sense!" exclaimed Magdalena. At least the why part of the mystery seemed to be solved.

"Um, I hate to be the bearer of unwelcome news, but werewolves chasing us and wanting to devour Magdalena isn't exactly what I would consider being good news," mumbled Hubert.

The smile quickly faded on Magdalena's face as Hubert's words seemed to materialize.

"You're right; I'm so sorry. My head is pounding, and I don't think I am thinking straight," whispered Magdalena. She didn't mean to trouble her friends with her problems but needed to explain her actions.

"Magdalena, is there anything we can do for you," asked Greta? She hated to see her friend in pain.

"Yeah, Greta, we can solve this mystery and get home!" grumbled Hubert.

"Oh, no, I'm okay. I just need Y'all to make sure my ideas are making logical sense. I must have taken a hard fall for this bump on my head is quite large."

"We've got you, Mags, don't worry," comforted Greta.

Piper looked up from his book and said, "I have a clue, guys!"

Everyone was staring at Piper in anticipation of what juicy information he had found.

"Werewolves are very loyal, and apparently they can't eat if something happens to their master until the playing field is leveled," read Piper.

"What does that suppose to mean?" asked Cody.

Piper continued reading out loud. "Therefore, if a werewolf's master is killed maliciously, the creature will go hungry until his master's death is avenged."

"Oh, my God! No, no, no, this can't be happening. Are you kidding me?" panicked Hubert.

Gabriel was pretty much at a loss for words. This most definitely wasn't something he wanted to hear.

Magdalena looked as white as a ghost. Her hands were beginning to tremble, and she realized why she had been locked up in that stone dungeon cellar. She was supposed to starve to death, just like the werewolves. She was the one responsible for removing the demons from Lily Brooke, and the one responsible for the werewolves' curse of starvation. Well, all three heads of the one werewolf, she surmised. If her friends hadn't of rescued her, the plight would be the same as the three-headed creature's.

"So, how do we escape and get out of here, first. Second, what do we do about this starving werewolf problem? I mean, as soon as we get home, they are going to hunt us down. They already found us at the campsite. It won't take them long to find out where all of us live. How do we permanently get rid of them?" inquired Cody.

"Hang on, guys," said Piper. "I may have something."

Gabriel had walked over to Magdalena and was reading the text over her shoulder while everyone was discussing the issues at hand. He knew her focus was the sharpest it could be with everything she had gone through tonight, so he was reading ahead trying to learn more about King and Queen Lindtzl in case she happened to miss something.

"I've got it!" shouted Piper. "I know how we can destroy the werewolves forever."

"Do tell!" shouted Greta.

"So, they go hungry until they avenge their demon master's death, right? It says here that if they eat for any reason before justice has been served, they will instantly die, and the spell is broken."

"Woah! So, all we need to do is feed them, and the curse is broken, and they die, and we are safe again? Why does that sound too easy?" asked Hubert.

"Yep! According to this book, that's it," responded Piper.

Gabriel looked up from the book he had been reading over Magdalena's shoulder.

"There is more, guys," he said.

All eyes now turned to Gabriel in anticipation.

"According to legend, when King Lindtzl died in the attack, the queen became a hermit. She was deeply in love with her king and couldn't get past the grief of his passing. The dungeon tunnels were built as a precaution to any future attack, and security measures were placed throughout the castle to protect it from demons and werewolves that roamed The Enchanted Forest."

"So, the queen had the four tunnels built for safety. Tunnel number one is obvious, you get locked up in there, and you starve to death and die of isolation. Tunnel number two is directly across from the stone steps leading upstairs to the castle foyer. We don't know what is in tunnel number two. Tunnel number three, we are sitting in it. It appears to provide a hidden meeting place, warmth, and all these books full of history. Tunnel number four, who knows?" surmised Gabriel.

"That sounds about right," said Magdalena. "So, if we go with Piper's information and find a way to feed the werewolves, we can defeat the curse! But, with all the booby traps and security measures the queen had installed in the castle, how can we get out of here safely?"

"Although I know this won't be a popular option, we may need to explore tunnels number two and four to understand what we are dealing with here. It is possible there will be a hidden escape," said Cody.

Gabriel stood lost in thought for a moment. Although he didn't embrace Cody's suggestion for obvious reasons, he did, however, think Cody may be correct. There were so many unknowns in the castle; one wrong move could mean death. While he stood there debating back and forth with himself, Magdalena cleared her throat and addressed the group.

"Okay, guys, Cody is probably right. This castle is booby-trapped everywhere with hidden tunnels, rotating walls, pits of skeletons, and light-activated motion triggers. And, that is just what we KNOW about already. I can't even begin to imagine what we have yet to discover. So, although I agree with Cody, I have an idea that may get us home safely sooner than later."

There wasn't a MALB member in that room that wasn't anxiously awaiting Magdalena's next comment. If she had figured out a way to get them safely home, they were all ears.

THREE-HEADED WEREWOLF

~ Eight ~

Hubert stood in anticipation of Magdalena's plan. There was nothing on the face of this earth that he wanted or needed more than getting the heck out of this miserable nightmare.

"Okay, guys, listen closely. My plan is dependent upon us working seamlessly together," whispered Magdalena.

All children walked over in front of the warmth glowing from the fireplace and took a seat on the floor. Everyone sat cross-legged in a circle, leaning in close to each other, while they listened intently to Magdalena's plan. It took quite a bit of explaining, but once she had wrapped it up, everyone started feeling much better than they had up to this point.

Gabriel knew that if anyone could pull this off, it was Mags. But, he did have to admit there was very little room for error. One wrong move and the hungry beast could eat them alive, or worse, he gulped.

Hubert took charge of the meeting and cleared his throat.

"Let's take a vote. Everyone, say 'I' as I go around the room if you agree to Magdalena's plan. If not, say 'nay.'"

As Hubert went around the room, he confirmed all six 'I's to include his very own.

"It's confirmed! We have a lot of work to do, so let's get started!" exclaimed Hubert.

The plan was very detailed, and Magdalena knew it would have to come together like a perfect storm to be successful. But she knew based on their last adventure, that when the going got tough, MALB worked like a well-oiled machine, together!

There were three parts to the plan: part A, part B, and part C. Once A was completed, the group knew to move on to B, etc., quickly... So, without further ado, everyone rose to their feet to get started.

Cody and Piper were responsible for distracting the three-headed beast in tunnel number one, while Greta and Magdalena escaped up the stone staircase that led from the underground dungeons to the castle foyer. Gabriel and Hubert were going to explore tunnel number four. Once Cody and Piper had led the creature to tunnel number one and hopefully trapped it, they would scurry to tunnel number two and take a quick glance. In theory, everyone would meet back at The Enchanted Forest sign.

Everyone stood tall as they prayed the rotating wall worked on the inside of the hidden conference room. Cody and Piper approached the wall and gave it a light push. There were no handles, levers, or anything noticeable on the inside of the room. Luckily, the wall gave a small turn giving just the ample amount of space needed for everyone to squeeze out of the room and back into the tunnel.

Once everyone had vacated the hidden room, Cody and Piper gently closed the faux fireplace wall. They all stood there just a moment, marveling at how nothing could be detected from the inside of the tunnel. Queen Lindtzl must have been one very smart lady.

Magdalena and Greta approached the bottom of the staircase and ducked down, flattening their bodies as much as possible against the wall at the bottom of the stairs. They planned to crouch in the darkness without being detected as the werewolf creature came flying down the stairs. Hopefully, Cody and Piper would cause enough of a distraction that the werewolf and its three heads wouldn't notice the girls.

Gabriel and Hubert headed off further into the castle's bowels towards tunnel number four. Hubert, of course, was terrified. But he knew if they didn't find all the clues they needed, they would have to return to Lindtzl Castle. And, that just wasn't something he wanted to do, ever again.

Within a few moments, both Gabriel and Hubert were out of sight. It was now time for Cody and Piper to create that distraction.

As Greta and Magdalena lay flat against the stone-cold wall, they heard Cody and Piper begin. The girls could hear the guys banging on the wooden door yelling for help, as loudly as they could. From where the girls were standing, you could most definitely tell the noise was coming from tunnel number one.

Sure enough, the three-headed werewolf heard the ruckus. Before the girls could even flinch, the stench could be smelled in the air. The beast had begun the ten-minute descent to the castle dungeon.

The sound of running hooves, stinky breath, and just plain evil ambiance was headed straight for the basement cellar. At this point, there was no other way out of the situation they had all become entrapped. The only exit was the staircase that the beast was currently descending.

Both Magdalena and Greta closed their eyes as the beast neared the bottom of the stairs and held their breath.

Just as Magdalena had hoped, the beast knew which tunnel it would find Cody and Piper and didn't even glance towards the wall that Greta and Magdalena had plastered themselves against.

The wind whipped through their hair as the animal made a sharp right turn at the bottom of the steps. Magdalena opened her eyes long enough to see the monstrosity of the animal galloping down tunnel number one towards her friends.

Before she could blink, Greta found herself flying up the dungeon steps with Magdalena softly pulling her along. The climb was brutal as both girls never lost sight of the fact that the beast could turn around at any moment and find them.

The girls climbed as fast as they could put one foot in front of the other. Greta thought her heart was going to beat out of her chest, literally. Magdalena was determined to get to that foyer before anything could stop her. As they reached the top step, Magdalena and Greta tripped and landed on the foyer floor. Both stunned, they lie face down on the stone floor. Magdalena was fairly certain she had busted her lip as the taste of hot blood flooded her mouth.

Holding hands, the girls scrambled to their feet, both dazed and frightened for their lives, and faced the drawbridge door in front of them. As they stood there eyeing the exit, Magdalena wondered how they were going to open the door.

Meanwhile, Cody and Piper were inside of the dungeon cell, where Magdalena had been held captive. Both were hiding behind the opened door where the skeleton had once laid to frighten Magdalena.

They could hear the three-headed beast coming down tunnel number one. It sounded like an army of werewolves, not one lone creature. Both boys knew there was no room for mistakes. They had to execute exactly how Magdalena had planned it out for them. They stood there waiting, anticipating the moment they would stare eyeballs to eyeballs with the demonic gatekeepers. Within moments, the time arrived.

The demonic beast jumped the skeleton pit and landed in the middle of the room. All three heads were frantically moving in different directions, their eyes scanning the room for the imposters. Cody looked at Piper and mouthed one…two…three!

Together, with everything they could muster, Cody and Piper came from behind the wooden door, jumped around it, and over the open skeleton pit landing on the other side of the pit, but sprawled on the tunnel floor. The loud bang could be heard throughout the dungeon, and it seemed the walls shook.

Half anticipating the beast to launch itself and land on top of them, Cody and Piper slowly opened their eyes. There, in front of them, stood the now-closed solid wooden door with small iron grate peep- window. They did it!

Both boys lie on the ground giggling in extreme hysteria. Magdalena's plan had so far worked! The beast was trapped inside of the same cell, where Magdalena had been left to starve to death.

As the boys remained there reveling in the fact the plan had worked, the three-headed werewolf began violently howling and shaking the door from inside of the dungeon cell.

In fear, they quickly decided it was time to get moving. They ran down tunnel number one and arrived at the base of the stone steps. Magdalena and Greta were nowhere to be found. Realizing the girls must have escaped, Cody and Piper began the steep incline up the hundreds of stone stairs.

In the intensity of the moment, exploring tunnel number two was just not an option. Who knew how long the door between the werewolf and MALB would last before the beast successfully tore it down.

So, they climbed for what felt like an eternity. As they reached the top step and crossed over into the castle foyer, the boys saw Greta and Magdalena standing in front of them, looking defeated.

Gabriel and Hubert were now near the end of tunnel number four. Hubert had sweat trickling down the side of his head even though it was cold and drafty in the dark, castle dungeon tunnels. His nerves were on edge, and he knew it. There, in front of the two boys, stood a locked door. Gabriel grabbed the doorknob and tried to turn it clockwise and then reverse. But, it was to no avail.

"What now?" inquired Hubert. "Gabriel, what if this room holds clues we need to get back home?"

Gabriel didn't like this dead-end any more than Hubert did.

"I don't know, Hubert. Let me think!" exclaimed Gabriel.

Gabriel was frantically trying to come up with an idea, but nothing was materializing for him. Worried sick, he sat on the ground with his back to the locked dungeon door.

Hubert had never witnessed Gabriel so deflated. He sat down beside his friend and searched for anything he could say to help Gabriel come up with a solution.

"What would Mags do?" asked Hubert. "If Magdalena came to a dead end with a locked door, what would she do?"

Gabriel sat, contemplating Hubert's words. He didn't know the answers to his questions, but he knew the one thing Magdalena would not do is give up.

"You're right, Hubert. We need to think about what Magdalena would do," said Gabriel. "She would keep trying something, anything!"

With that last thought, Gabriel stood up and turned the doorknob again; it remained locked. He then gave a little nudge, and instead of trying to open the door with the knob, he tried to push it open. Bingo! The door opened slightly, allowing them passage inside of whatever lies on the other side of the door.

Gabriel and Hubert exchanged glances. How genius Queen Lindtzl must have been to have a door appear to be locked when all you had to do was push it open!

"I don't know about you, Gabriel, but I think we should use light to scan the room before we go inside," suggested Hubert.

"Good idea, let's go," responded Gabriel as he pulled his flashlight back out of his jacket pocket.

Gabriel shined the light from floor to ceiling as he and Hubert leaned up against the partially opened dungeon door. Cobwebs littered the room, and a musty texture and dampness were noticeable.

"This place gives me the creeps," said Hubert.

"Agreed," replied Gabriel. "This room feels much mustier and damp, more abandoned than the conference room tunnel."

"I seriously don't want to know why," whined Hubert. Although, in his deepest of gut instincts, he knew he was about to find out why.

"Watch your step and go slow," whispered Gabriel as he stepped completely inside of the musty room.

"Oh, don't worry," replied Hubert as he followed Gabriel inside. The door remained partially opened, which Hubert figured was probably a false sense of security.

The two boys cautiously began exploring the room, one step at a time. It appeared to be an empty room full of vines, spider webs, and tree roots. The ambiance was weird, something between a cross of a deserted jungle and a basement cellar.

Gabriel got on his knees to inspect one of the massive tree roots closer. Hubert crouched down beside Gabriel, as the last thing he wanted was to be standing up alone in case that three-headed werewolf came running at them.

As the boys were touching and inspecting the huge tree roots, they noticed just behind them was a hole in the ground. Gabriel leaned over the opening and shined his flashlight to get a better view of what could be below.

"It looks like an old water well," said Hubert. "That would make sense as to why the musty mildew feels in this creepy room."

"Yeah, I think you are right," said Gabriel. "But, I wonder where these large tree roots are coming from."

Before either one of them could venture another guess, the large root closest to Gabriel's foot reached up, wrapped itself around both the boys' waists, and scooped them up off the ground. Hubert and Gabriel were screaming for dear life. They were being flung all around the musty room, flying through the air and trapped in the grasp of the enchanted tree root.

"Gabriel, do something!" shouted Hubert. "This tree root is squeezing the breath out of me! I don't want to die at the hands of a haunted tree!"

Gabriel was holding on as tightly as he could. He had been caught completely off guard and couldn't even speak.

Cody, Piper, Magdalena, and Greta could hear the screams of their two friends all the way up the staircase inside of the castle foyer.

"Oh, my gosh! That is Gabriel and Hubert screaming!" shouted Greta.

"Quick! We have to save them!" shouted Magdalena. "We can't leave them here!"

Within seconds, the four MALB members were running back down the stone steps as fast as they could.

So much for escaping, thought Greta.

They were so close to getting out of Lindtzl Castle and meeting at the forest sign. As a matter of fact, it had been so close she could still taste it.

As the friends descended the steps, each one of them silently prayed the three-headed werewolf hadn't yet escaped. Otherwise, this day was going to go from bad to worse.

As they reached the last step, they could hear the werewolf pounding on the door in the dungeon cellar, so they quickly turned left, running towards tunnel number four. The friends were not sure what they would find once they got there, but knew no matter what they faced, leaving their friends in need was simply not an option.

Magdalena had her flashlight illuminating the tunnel, and as they neared the end of it, she could see the door was cracked open. As all four of them reached the door, they took a deep breath and slid into the room while hugging the wall. Before they could even blink, a huge tree root came swinging in front of them, scooped them all up, and before they could grasp what had happened, was tossed into the air with Hubert and Gabriel.

The only thing any of them could hear was each other's screams. At this point, they were all completely out of options and at the mercy of the enchanted tree roots.

Time seemed to stand still as everyone began to feel sick to their stomach from the flipping, tossing, and turning. Gabriel thought for sure they were going to all die from shaken syndrome.

Suddenly, the tree roots violently threw all six of them down the open well. They seemed to be falling, almost suspended in time. The well was very deep, and the friends could feel the damp, wet air as they fell through debris, tree branches, cobwebs, and moss.

Magdalena remembered the locket that hung around her neck. She knew she had to act quickly to save their lives. She grasped the locket, closed her eyes, and screamed at the top of her lungs for everyone to try and grab hands. They were all in a free fall, flipping in different directions but somehow managed to grab hands while descending into the unknown abyss.

Now, time for a little black magic, she thought.

BLACK MAGIC

~ Nine ~

Magdalena grasped her locket in her left hand while holding hands with Greta on the other. She closed her eyes and knew she had to get this right.

"Lily root, lily root, agent of the night, save us from free fall, give us wings of an angel to fly through the night!" prayed Magdalena.

Before anyone could speak or think, the six friends began to float through the open abyss slowly. Their speed dramatically decreased, and they almost seemed suspended in time.

Magdalena's spell had worked! The lily root was stopping their free fall. It was as though someone or something had wrapped their arms around the six friends and were carrying them softly to the ground below.

Within a few moments, MALB softly landed on the cold, wet ground. Shivering from nerves and the damp air, they all stood looking at each other with hands still held.

"You saved our lives, Magdalena. That was amazing!" shouted Hubert. He couldn't believe

Magdalena was able to think so quickly, as they were falling to their potential death below in the bottom of the deep well.

"The lily root saved our lives, Hubert. But I'm just glad I had it with me! I can't help but think what would have happened without it!" exclaimed Magdalena.

Still feeling a little woozy and shaken up, Gabriel tried to steady his voice as he spoke. "Mags, never in a million years can I ever repay you. We did it this time. If the four of you had already left the castle and headed to the forest sign, Hubert and I would be laying on the ground of this well."

Magdalena knew her friends understood well how dire the outcome would have been if she, Greta, Cody, and Piper had already escaped the castle before the enchanted tree roots had captured Hubert and Gabriel.

"Well, guys, again, I hate to be the bearer of any bad news, but we are stuck in the bottom of an old well, in an enchanted forest with no exit," said Hubert.

The six friends started exploring the deep well they found themselves stranded in, trying to find any possible exit. Finding absolutely nothing, they sat on the cold, wet ground, feeling beaten.

"There is no way out," cried Hubert. "We are stuck here forever!"

Although Hubert's words felt dramatic, Greta had to admit to herself quietly he was probably right.

"What if Mags," began Gabriel, "What if you used the lily root to fly us back up the well into tunnel number four again?"

"Are you crazy, man? Those enchanted tree roots were going to kill us! There is no way I can survive all that tossing around again," replied Hubert.

Magdalena was giving Gabriel's words some thought.

"What if I used the lily root to fly us back up to tunnel number four, but I cast a spell somehow that would put the tree roots in a deep sleep. Maybe that would give us enough time to get out of that tunnel and back into the castle foyer before the three-headed werewolf finds us again," suggested Magdalena.

"I like it!' shouted Cody. "I mean, I don't want to go anywhere near that castle again, but right now, we are in the bottom of an empty well inside of the castle dungeon. Nowhere to go from here, but up!"

Magdalena looked around her and saw that all her friends liked the idea compared to being stranded in the bottom of a spooky well.

"Okay, we are going to do this in the same manner. Everyone, grab hands, and I'm going to work some black magic. Be sure not to break hands. It is very important! If anyone breaks the grip, then that person will be on his or her own and sadly will be left behind," warned Magdalena.

They all grabbed hands, and Hubert held on especially tight. As a matter of fact, Greta felt sure he was about to break her hand. Magdalena closed her eyes and began the spell.

"Lily root, lily root, agent of the night! Save us all from the depths of despair, raise us into the night away from our plight," demanded Magdalena. "Put the enchantments to sleep, deep into the night, keep their wicked roots at bay until we stop flight."

Immediately, the six friends began to softly float through the air, climbing higher and higher towards the top of the open well. Time seemed to stand still, as MALB slowly inched towards the top of the musty well. Once they reached the top, they were able to climb out of the well onto their hands and knees. As they stood up, they noticed the tree roots seemed frozen, almost dead. The black magic had worked! The tree roots were in a deep sleep.

Not wanting to wake them, or worse end the spell, the six friends ran outside of the wicked room and closed the door behind them.

Standing there in the dark tunnel, everyone tried to catch their breath. Greta had her flashlight on and could see the fear in all their eyes. They had just survived one of the most intense and scary moments of their lives.

"Now what?" whispered Greta. "Do we go back to the foyer? We didn't see a way out!"

"Wait, what?" asked Gabriel. "What do you mean, you didn't see a way out? Couldn't you open the drawbridge door and escape?"

"No, that's just it, Gabriel. The reason we heard you and Hubert calling for help is we were stuck in the castle foyer. The drawbridge door was closed shut with no foreseeable way to open it!" exclaimed Magdalena.

Gabriel and Hubert glanced at each other, both silently thinking the same thing. Their friends saved their lives, but now they were all six trapped inside of this weird and wicked castle.

"Great. After all of that, we just endured, we are all still trapped. Will it ever end? What now?" asked Hubert.

"Let's think about this, guys. The castle foyer seems to be completely blocked. Tunnel number one was a no go. It has a very upset three-headed werewolf inside of that cell. Tunnel number three is nothing more than a hidden sanctuary conference room. Tunnel number four nearly killed us with enchanted tree roots and an empty well. That only leaves us with tunnel number two. But if it goes like all the rest of the tunnels have gone, it won't have an exit, and Lord knows what will be found inside of it," reasoned Gabriel.

"Yeah, we decided not to check it out after we caged the beast," said Cody. "We were afraid we wouldn't have time to escape the castle as who knows what is in that tunnel!"

His words rang true for everyone. No matter how they twisted the scenario, thought about their options, and brainstormed, they always came back to the one issue. So far, there was no way out. They had no other option than to try tunnel number two. All other avenues had been a failure.

Taking a deep breath, Magdalena faced her friends in that dark, eerie tunnel.

"We have got to figure something out very soon. The werewolf will find a way to break free before too much longer. We haven't even accomplished part A of our plan to get back home! We have no choice. We absolutely have to explore tunnel number two, and pray we find something that helps us instead of trying to kill us."

You could hear the round of moans coming from the other five MALB members. No one wanted to explore anything; they just wanted to go home. But without a way out of Lindtzl Castle, no one was escaping anywhere.

"You're right, Mags. We are just all tired and sleepy. Come on, guys, we can do this," comforted Gabriel.

"Yes, we have to do this, guys," responded Cody. He also wanted nothing more than a warm cup of hot chocolate, a snuggly sleeping bag, and a nice campfire. But on the contrary, he would settle for not being eaten by a three-headed werewolf, strangled by an enchanted tree root, or left for dead in a hidden dungeon cell littered with bones.

"Let's go, guys!" shouted Gabriel as he led the way to tunnel number two.

As the children reached the end of tunnel number two, there stood another locked door in front of them. Realizing that nothing was as it seemed inside of this enchanted castle, Gabriel tried turning the doorknob clockwise, and then counter-clockwise, but to no avail. He then gave a slight nudge to try and open the door. He noticed as he touched the steel door, it was freezing. Gabriel jumped back as he noticed his hands were almost frostbitten. *How could that happen*, he wondered?

"What's wrong, Gabriel?" inquired Greta.

"The door is freezing!" exclaimed Gabriel. The perplexed look on his face said it all. *Here we go again*, they all thought.

FROSTBITE

~ Ten ~

Who would have ever thought you could get frostbitten inside of a castle? As Gabriel examined his hand, he realized he needed to get it warmed up quickly. He could feel the pain beginning to run from his hand up through his elbow. Magdalena took her pink scarf off her neck and wrapped it around Gabriel's hand.

"Hopefully, this will help," said Magdalena. "I'm so sorry, Gabriel. This entire castle is one trick after another. Who would have ever thought this door would be frozen!"

"It's okay, Mags; it's beginning to feel better with the scarf wrapped around it. I'm sure as it warms up, it will be just fine. But what a clever idea that Queen Lindtzl had to deter others from this door."

Magdalena sat lost in thought for a few moments. Gabriel could be on to something. If Queen Lindtzl didn't want anyone to pay any attention to this tunnel room, this was an effective way to accomplish it. For werewolves, it would take one lick of the doorknob or door, and their tongues would be frozen. That wouldn't happen many times before the animals steered clear of this door.

"I think we may have found our exit!" exclaimed Magdalena.

"Wait, did I miss something, Mags?" inquired Hubert. "We have a locked and frozen door, and you think we have found our exit? Have you gone mad?"

Cody and Piper were doing that thing again, where they stare at each other and have a complete conversation with body language. They were both very confused, even more so than Hubert, apparently. Greta just stood there staring into space as though her mind was a million miles away.

"Think about it, guys! When you landed from the slide down the slippery slope, you said there was a frozen pond right beside you. As a matter of fact, the puddle you found that transported you through the hidden vortex to get to The Enchanted Forest, was still liquid. Since it wasn't frozen, you noticed the oddity and looked closer at the puddle. Right?" asked Magdalena.

"Yes, the pond was frozen, yet the puddle was not," responded Hubert. "I fell into the puddle by slipping, and that is how we discovered the vortex."

"Precisely! And you said that when the vortex ended, you landed in a dirt tunnel somewhere underneath the frozen pond. You followed that path and wound up in a clearing inside of The Enchanted Forest," reminded Magdalena.

"Yes, Mags, but what does all of that have to do with this frozen door?" asked Cody.

"Well, I am willing to bet that Queen Lindtzl was one tough cookie! She created a hidden vortex to escape the castle without detection quickly, that would get her out of The Enchanted Forest before anyone knew she was gone!" replied Magdalena.

As the other five MALB members stood there clinging to Magdalena's every word, the details were beginning to come together for them, slowly. The connection of the frozen pond and frozen steel door at the end of tunnel number two couldn't be a coincidence. The frozen door was completely out of context. It had to be a sign that would remind the queen which tunnel was her escape. It now made so much sense that the six of them were in awe.

"Queen Lindtzl was a genius!" shouted Piper. "Pure genius!"

The excitement was quickly beginning to pick up as each MALB member was piecing the puzzle back together quickly.

"So, tunnel number one and tunnel number four, the outlying tunnels, are traps! They are meant for punishment and security measures for trespassers. Tunnels number two and three are safe havens for the queen and her staff if needed. Tunnel number three gives them warmth, history, books that provide any information needed for generations to come. Tunnel number two, we pray, leads out of Lindtzl Castle, out of The Enchanted Forest, and back to the frozen pond!" exclaimed Gabriel. "Mags, you are a pure genius!"

"Well, everyone, do not get too excited before we get to the other side of that frozen steel door. I could be wrong. All the pieces seem as though they make logical sense, but the one thing we have learned through all our adventures is this world we are standing in is enchanted. There are different playbook rules," warned Magdalena.

"Yes, you are right. Everyone, be sure to keep your wits about you. We think we have this figured out, but only time will tell," replied Piper.

"So, let's assume that we can enter the frozen door, and it leads us back to the frozen pond above The Enchanted Forest. We had to slide down the slippery slope to get to the pond. How in the world will we ever get back up to the cliff?" asked Hubert.

Everyone could feel their moods drop about two octaves. Hubert had a really good point.

"Let's cross one bridge at a time. Think about it, guys. The information we find behind this door will lead us to the next clue," responded Magdalena.

All heads nodded in agreement.

"So, if the door is locked and doesn't push open, how do we get in?" asked Greta.

"Think about it," responded Magdalena. "Queen Lindtzl was ahead of her time. All her booby traps and hidden access points in this castle, at least those we have discovered, are activated using light and heat. The queen most definitely possessed a sense of humor. We use our flashlights to defrost the doorknob! I am betting it won't turn, not because it is locked, but because it is frozen! That is why Gabriel's hand has frostbite," stated Magdalena proudly.

"Wow, I would have never gotten there," mumbled Cody. "Great work, Magdalena. Let's give it a try!"

Everyone pulled out their flashlights and began concentrating the light source directly on the door now. Within a few moments, they could see the frost begin to melt as the water was dripping down the length of the door.

After about five minutes of concentrating the light around the doorknob, Gabriel gave it a turn using the scarf wrapped hand. Sure enough, the door opened! Not sure what they would find on the other side of the now semi-frozen steel door, MALB began mentally preparing themselves for whatever evil was to come.

WINTER WONDERLAND

~ Eleven ~

As Gabriel pushed open the door, none of the children were expecting the sight that lay before them. It was nothing short of magical. It was an enchanted winter wonderland. As they all crossed the threshold, no one gave a second thought to the door they closed behind them. They had found paradise, or the winter version of it anyway. The friends all began to giggle with excitement as they saw the winter delight before them.

"Wow, do you guys see this? This is nuts?! How does this happen in a wicked, enchanted castle full of crazy three-headed creatures, booby traps, and all that other spooky stuff that has happened to us tonight?" inquired Hubert.

No one even attempted a response as they were still trying to process the goodness they saw in front of them. Magdalena couldn't help but feel proud of all of them. They had been faced with such dark and traumatic events tonight, yet here they stood in the middle of the most complete magic wonderland they had ever seen. The snow was glistening white and sparkled everywhere you looked. Christmas lights were hung around every tree. Large Christmas ornament bulbs, garland, and pine cones graced every evergreen tree within sight. Birds were chirping the songs of the holiday season. The scene before them was one out of a picture book. As wonderful and amazing as the holiday celebration had been in Lily Brooke's town square, nothing compared to the sight before them now.

The children began running around in circles and trying to catch snowflakes on their tongues. The bliss they felt now was much needed and such a treat, compared to the anxiety and fear they had dealt with all night. This just couldn't be true.

"Guys, this is amazing, but we need to get going! As wonderful as this place truly seems, we need to complete part A of our plan and get back home soon!" reminded Gabriel.

Knowing Gabriel was right, all six of the friends began following the trail leading off into the distance. As they walked for about ten minutes or so, they came upon a quaint area near the frozen pond. There was a twelve-foot white picnic table covered in food from one end to the other. Realizing how starving they were, the friends ran straight for the table.

As they reached the table of goodness, everyone sat down without another thought and began to devour the delicious meal in front of them. There were candied carrots, baked caramelized brussel sprouts, tender prime rib, cranberry sauce, mashed sweet potatoes, rolls, and more candy and cakes than they had ever seen in one spot. Magdalena was admiring the table centerpiece, a four-foot carved ice snow angel when they heard the jingle bells coming from around the corner.

The fear began to creep up through their souls as they realized that maybe this had all been one huge trap. Holding their breath, they sat frozen at the table, waiting on whom or what was coming from around the bend.

She was beautiful. Absolutely, positively, the most beautiful woman they had ever seen. She arrived in a buggy fit for a queen. Eight horses pulled the red velvet-lined buggy with evergreen wreaths hanging from their neck, sporting beautiful red, satin bows. The woman had long dark hair, almost black, with skin as ivory as snow. Her gown was made of glittery white satin and sparkled underneath the Christmas lights. It was the largest hoop skirt that Magdalena had ever seen. It looked like a ball gown made for a queen. She had never seen anything so magnificent in all her life.

As the woman descended from her carriage, she began walking slowly towards the children. She had helpers, as a matter of fact, there were about eight of them. Six of them stood guard by the carriage while the other two guards escorted the woman towards the table. Her smile was so sweet, and her lips were cherry red. She was flawless, and it helped the friends remain calm as they had no idea who she was, or what was about to happen.

"Greetings, my children. I see you were hungry and found the spread of food that I instructed my staff to prepare for you. I hope you have found everything to your liking. Especially you, Hubert, I know you are a food connoisseur, so I hope you have found the recipes to be acceptable?" inquired the woman.

Hubert sat unable to say a word, as he was feeling something between gratitude for the food and awe, for he had never seen a woman as beautiful as the one standing before him.

The rest of MALB tried to find their manners and began shaking their heads, yes.

"Hello mam, thank you kindly on all of our behalfs for your graciousness," whispered Magdalena. "You must forgive us, as we are unsure of where we are, who you are, and we have had quite the intense and scary night."

"Yes, yes, my child. Please forgive my manners. I forget living here in this wonderland that we are removed from mainstream society, and no one knows who we are," smiled the woman. "My dears, I am Queen Lindtzl and am pleased to make your acquaintance."

No one could speak. The six children sat in utter shock, with the queen standing right in front of them. No one knew whether to drop to their knees and bow, or cry, or praise the Lord!

"Oh, my goodness, we have never met a queen before!" exclaimed Magdalena.

Magdalena jumped up from her seat at the table and quickly kneeled before the queen. Her five friends quickly followed her lead, and all of them were knee down in the snow, giving thanks to the queen.

"Your majesty, thank you so much for feeding us. Your home here is absolutely beautiful!" said Magdalena.

"Thank you, my dears. I caught wind of the fact a group of children had found themselves in The Enchanted Forest. I have been praying for your safety as the beasts have taken over Lindtzl Castle," responded the queen.

"Yes, mam, there is an awful three-headed werewolf that attacked me and left me stranded in a dungeon cell. If it weren't for my friends, I would have died alone and starved in the cellar room," cried Magdalena. The fear was quickly coming back, even being surrounded in the white goodness around her.

"Don't worry, my child, you are safe now. The werewolves sabotaged my late husband's carriage many years ago, and he passed away. I know all too well how savage the werewolves can be," replied the queen.

"You see, The Enchanted Forest is just that, enchanted. And many years ago, all enchanted beings to include witches, wizards, demons, werewolves, and pure humans, lived together in harmony. Something upset that harmony, and we never figured out just what happened. But we used to travel through The Enchanted Forest at night, with no problems. Then one night, my husband was visiting a friend, and he took the royal carriage back home to Lindtzl Castle. For an unknown reason, the werewolves attacked the carriage, killed my husband, and went into hiding," explained the queen.

"Oh, Queen Lindtzl, we read about that night in one of the books we found in the hidden conference room, in tunnel number three inside of the castle dungeon," said Greta.

"Yes, I had it documented in book form, so if anything ever happened to me, someone in the future would know why the castle is now booby-trapped. After that night, to stay as safe as possible, I had the underground tunnel system designed. The two outlying tunnels are meant for no one to survive them. They are wicked, and the hope was anything demonic would be trapped there forever. Tunnel number three was an escape within the castle. It was meant to be somewhere that my staff and I could convene for a short amount of time if the castle were invaded. It is where we would strategize. Tunnel number two was to be used for the need to evacuate. We knew the demons and werewolves wouldn't be able to figure out how to open the door. Their tongues and hands would freeze, and other than using light and heat, the door is impenetrable," explained Queen Lindtzl.

"The werewolves used tunnel number one as retribution against Magdalena," said Hubert. "And all six of us almost died between the wicked tree roots that tried to squeeze us to death and the fall to the bottom of the musty well."

"Oh, my, I'm so glad you survived. The castle wasn't meant to harm children, only the wicked and demonic forces of evil," whispered the queen. "But how did you find The Enchanted Forest, and why are the werewolves after you?"

Gabriel took a deep breath and began the story that started about three months ago, on that fateful night. The queen was intensely interested, and she took a seat at the head of the buffet table so that she could hear more.

"So, you mean to tell me, the werewolves are seeking retribution against Magdalena because she is a *chosen one* that entrapped their masters?" asked the queen.

"Yes, we believe so," replied Magdalena. "The Grand Demon fell in love with my mother many years ago, back when she used to live amongst the witches and wizards of Lily Brooke. But my mother, Leona Gottschalk, didn't return that love. She had fallen deeply in love with my father, Paulos Gottschalk, who is a pure human. This enraged the Grand Demon, and the revolt began. The good witches and wizards that used to live in harmony with the citizens of Lily Brooke were tired of the demon's wicked ways. So, they left the clan and began marrying and living amongst pure humans in the community. This angered the Grand Demon on such a level that it unleashed a war between the demonic world and Lily Brooke."

"My, my, that sure sums it up for me," responded Queen Lindtzl. "That must be why after years of living harmoniously, the demons and their gatekeepers, the werewolves, began attacking citizens in our kingdom of Lindtzl. And, my king," she said sadly.

"I'm so sorry, Queen Lindtzl. I feel as though this is somehow my fault," cried Magdalena. She could feel a tear begin to trickle down the side of her face.

"Oh, my child, none of this is your fault, or your mother's fault, or anyone else's fault. Where evil exists, evil will be felt," explained the queen. "Sometimes, terrible things happen to wonderful people, and in those times, we must find comfort from above."

Magdalena knew the queen was right. If anyone was to blame, it was the demon leadership of the demonic world. They were the ones that had made a choice to no longer live in harmony. They were greedy, wicked, and looked out for no one but themselves.

Magdalena continued the story.

"The war ended when Lily Brooke defeated the demons by entrapping the three demon heads of the clan into an enchanted symbol. The Grand Demon and his two chief leaders were all three locked inside a hidden lantern. Since that time, Lily Brooke has lived peacefully. Well, until my spiritual hearing manifested itself on my thirteenth birthday. My friends and I decided to go exploring in the woods behind Hubert's barn, and I began to hear these mumbling voices and shrill noises. Of course, we were curious and decided to explore further. That brings you back to where Gabriel began the story. We unleashed the demons. So, the werewolves are after me because they can't eat before justice is served," sighed Magdalena.

"Hmm, I may have an idea for you," responded the queen.

All eyes turned to face the grace and beauty of Queen Lindtzl.

PRIME RIB

~ Twelve ~

Queen Lindtzl whispered to MALB her plan, and everyone became more excited by the moment. Magdalena's plan A had worked; they had escaped the wicked castle. Now with the help of the queen, Plan B was in the planning stages. They needed to find a way to destroy the three-headed beast before returning to Lily Brooke, as the last thing they needed or wanted was the creature coming to seek them out in their small-town community. Even though approximately thirty town members were part of a secret society made up of witches and wizards who looked over and protected the interests of Lily Brooke, none of them knew that one of the children, Magdalena, was a *chosen one*. And as far as Magdalena was concerned, it would stay that way. They had saved Lily Brooke once from the demons without any adults learning their secret, and this time would be no different.

A few moments later, the plan was complete, and now all the children had to do was execute exactly how the queen had instructed. If everything went well, the three-headed gatekeeper would be long gone, releasing the castle itself from all the evil these past several decades. The queen would be able to open the door to tunnel number two and enjoy the kingdom of Lindtzl, her castle, and the winter wonderland, all as one land. This idea excited the queen more than she could fathom as she missed her home dearly. As wonderful as the winter wonderland had been, she wanted to go home and be where her last happy days with the king had been lived. And, she wanted to regain control of the kingdom and bring happiness back to the land. For you see, an enchanted world could be fun and exciting, and it was only the dark and demonic forces of revenge that had clouded the land.

So, with full bellies and warm clothes, thanks to the queen, the six members of MALB were ready to begin plan B. Magdalena was going to cast a spell over the last of the prime rib that they had enjoyed for their late-night meal. It smelled heavenly, and the queen knew the three-headed werewolf would not be able to resist the temptation. Once the werewolf ate, the curse would then be broken. Or, that was the main idea of the plan.

Magdalena grabbed her lily root in one hand and placed her other hand over the prime rib platter. She closed her eyes, and everything seemed to stop. The queen stood in awe, watching the child begin her black magic.

"Lily root, lily root, agent of the night! Tenderize, flavor, and deliciously saturate this prime rib. For the demonic werewolf is hungry, tantalize his senses, make no creature refuse your lure. Take away, take away the demon's curse, end-all evil in the name of Lily Brooke!" demanded Magdalena.

Everyone watched Magdalena as she seemed to come out of her trance. Gabriel always found it amazing to watch her when she was casting a spell. It was as though she entered a completely different dimension of time and space. And quite frankly, for all he knew, she probably did.

"Okay, guys, it is now up to us!" said Magdalena.

"Now remember, once you have completed the task at hand, return here to this table, and we will move on to plan C, getting you home!" stated the queen.

"Yes, mam!" shouted MALB in unison.

Magdalena scooped up the prime rib and platter in both of her arms as Gabriel led the way. Everyone fell in line, secretly praying their ruse would work. Hubert took up the back of the line again, and everyone knew why. With that sly smirk he always had on his face, he thought he was fooling everyone.

As the friends walked through the winter, wonderland headed back to the dreaded steel door, the silence was deafening. It had been quite the night, and everyone was weary. The contrast between the beauty of the white, winter wonderland, and the dark, eerie castle, was not lost on any of them. Magdalena's soul yearned for the light, for the uplifting spirit she detected in Queen Lindtzl. She prayed their endeavor would be successful, and before they knew it, they would find themselves basking in the light, fluffy, white snow, and eating lots of Christmas cookies.

MALB arrived at the now semi-frozen steel door and walked through the doorway. The tunnel was dark, and the walk seemed long to tunnel number one. They knew the three-headed beast could smell their arrival, as it began to howl. *At least it smelled good*, thought Magdalena.

As they neared the solid wooden door with the little iron grate window opening, all eyes looked up. They could see the hair of the werewolf oozing through the opening. One of the heads was frantically trying to peek through the hole. Not wanting to lose a hand in this process, Magdalena had devised a plan.

"Okay, everyone, follow my lead, and whatever you do, don't break the grip of hands!" whispered Magdalena.

She sat the platter of enchanted prime rib on the floor in front of the door. The werewolf was going crazy, trying to scratch its way through the door. Magdalena knew they didn't have long before the beast would find a way to escape. And then, she wasn't quite sure the aroma of the prime rib would overtake the aroma of six healthy children.

Once the platter was on the floor, everyone grabbed hands. Magdalena held her lily root locket in one hand, and Greta's hand with the other. She closed her eyes, and Gabriel noticed that odd-like trance state was creeping over her face again.

"Lily root, lily root, agent of the night! Transport this enchanted prime rib through the iron grate window, leading to the stone cellar of this tunnel, behind the wooden door! Your destination is the three-headed beast!" demanded Magdalena.

Everyone remained holding hands and opened their eyes just in time to see the prime rib float off the platter, up to the little window opening, and through the door. No one had to guess if it had worked because they could hear the creature devouring every ounce of the prime rib goodness. Thanking the Lord for His small blessings, the group stood with their eyes fixed on the wooden door, waiting to see if the spell had worked.

Within a few moments, no sound could be heard from the other side of the door. Knowing the time was now, Magdalena climbed onto Gabriel's shoulders with the help of her friends, and they got closer to the small window at the top of the door. As careful as she could, and praying with everything inside of her, Magdalena leaned over and peered into the stone cellar dungeon room. There in front of her very eyes, was the three-headed beast, sound asleep. The spell had worked! The creature had eaten every morsel of the prime rib. There was now just one test left. But surviving it would be key.

Magdalena climbed down from the top of Gabriel's shoulders, and they stepped away from the door. Everyone was curious to hear what Magdalena had seen, although they suspected everything had turned out okay.

"Well, what did you see?" asked Hubert. He couldn't stand it any longer.

"It worked," whispered Magdalena. "Well, at least the first phase worked. The creature ate every drop of the prime rib. So, in theory, it should have broken the curse. But, we won't know until we give it the full test. I'm scared guys, really, really, scared," whimpered Magdalena.

Gabriel gave Magdalena a heartfelt hug. He was as nervous as she was and didn't want to see anything happen to his best friend. But he also knew, the five of them would be standing there with their friend, ready to attack with the flashlights. No matter what, they all knew werewolves hated light. So, when they ran their test, if it didn't go as planned, they still had the light on their side.

"Okay, are you ready, Mags?" asked Gabriel.

"Yes, ready as I will ever be," she responded.

In tears, everyone leaned in and gave Magdalena a big group hug. They all loved her dearly and silently prayed this would work.

"I couldn't do this without all of you," whispered Magdalena. "This is a team effort, and I know you have my back, as I would have yours. Let's finish this so we can all go home without looking over our shoulders for the rest of our lives."

"Amen to that!" shouted Hubert. He was completely done with all this mysterious demon and werewolf stuff. Completely done!

"Agreed!" said Cody.

"Yeah, I'm ready to sleep in my own bed," said Piper.

Greta had tears trickling down her face and couldn't find her voice, so she just smiled sweetly at her childhood friend. The next few moments in time would either be the happiest or scariest of their lives.

Since Magdalena was the one the werewolf was after for revenge, she needed to be the one to make sure the curse had been lifted. And being a human carrot, was something she had never quite pictured herself as being. But that was exactly what she about to be.

"Alright guys, as I step forward and place my hand on this doorknob, be sure to have your flashlights ready!" exclaimed Magdalena.

The rest of MALB had already pulled out their flashlights and had them aimed at the door. There was no way they would allow some three-headed demonic beast attack, their beloved Magdalena.

"We are ready, Mags," replied Cody.

"Yes, we are all set. Let's go!" said Gabriel.

With that, Magdalena stepped forward and placed her hand on the doorknob. It had only been a few hours since she had been locked up on the other side of this door and felt she was going to die in that dark, stone cellar room. Now, she had to face her fears. It was time to awaken the beast!

HUMAN CARROT

~ Thirteen ~

Magdalena took a deep breath and slowly opened the door. She had mentally prepared herself to be attacked the second the door swung open. What she wasn't prepared for was the sight before her eyes. There on the floor was the three-headed werewolf sound asleep. She knew the creature was breathing, as she could see its chest rise and fall with each breath. She turned to look at the others, poised with their flashlights, ready to attack. For the next few seconds, Magdalena was fairly certain that the six of them had a complete conversation with just the raising of eyebrows and body movement. Everyone had the same response, flabbergasted! No one could believe the hideous creature was lying on the cold, stone floor fast asleep.

Magdalena crossed over the threshold and began to taunt the werewolf.

"Wake up, you hideous and demonic creature! Look at you now, belly is full, and you are lazily sleeping! I'm standing right in front of you, now get up!" shouted Magdalena.

As Magdalena stood there hovering over the wicked animal, its eyes began to open. First, she noticed head number one was stirring with its eyes opening. Then, she quickly noticed the other two heads were moving, and within the next few moments, all eyeballs were on her. Magdalena was not prepared for what happened next.

The creature began to get up slowly, almost crawling on its belly. Once it stood up on all four legs, with the three separate heads bobbing around, it scanned the room for any potential danger. Magdalena was ready to give it a dose of bright light. But the creature exhibited no tendency towards violence, at all. As a matter of fact, the werewolf sat down on its hind legs staring at Magdalena and wagging its tail. No one expected this outcome.

"Magdalena, this is crazy!" shouted Hubert. "It worked! The curse is broken!"

"Yay!" shouted Cody.

The rest of MALB, everyone but Magdalena, began celebrating right there in the cold dungeon cellar. Magdalena was too much in disbelief to react at all. So, she inched closer and locked eyes with one of the heads and outreached her hand to the creature. The werewolf was very submissive and gently lowered one of the heads, expecting for

Magdalena to pet it on top of its head. Trembling, but knowing this would be the ultimate test, Magdalena gently outstretched her hand and patted the werewolf on the one head. Its tail began to wag, and all demonic activity seemed to have disappeared and left the animal.

The flood of relief flew through that dungeon tunnel, and the screams, laughter, and excitement could be heard from outside of Lindtzl Castle. Gabriel ran towards Magdalena and swept her off her feet, hugging her high in the air.

Everyone was jumping up and down and shouting at the top of their lungs, "Evil has been beaten! We did it! Life can now go back to normal!"

Magdalena was so happy that she couldn't control her emotions. The tears were streaming down her face while Gabriel was tossing her around in air-born hugs. At least this time, being a human carrot had worked out after all. She was still slightly shaking from the adrenaline rush she had experienced, but it was not lost on her that no longer would she and her closest friends have to look over their shoulders constantly. The demonic gatekeepers that had set out to destroy her for retribution of entrapping their masters had been defeated. The curse over Magdalena and the rest of MALB had been broken.

It was time for MALB to return to the winter wonderland and to let Queen Lindtzl know that she could return to her kingdom and home. As the celebration began to wind down, the friends realized how weary and tired they were. It had been such a long and brutal night. They all wanted nothing more than to crawl back to their sleeping bags by the dwindling campfire.

"I don't know about y'all, but I'm ready for bed," mumbled Hubert. "We just defeated the last of the demons, so let's find a way to get back home."

"I second that!" exclaimed Greta. "My body is aching from head to toe, and Lord knows I need some sleep. I've had it!"

Gabriel grabbed Magdalena by the hand and whispered in her ear, "Let's go find the queen and get out of this enchanted land."

Magdalena smiled and whispered back, "Amen to that! My sleeping bag is calling my name."

The gang headed back down tunnel number one towards tunnel number two, where the frozen steel door stood open. Cody realized someone was following them, so he quickly turned around and shined his flashlight. There, standing a few feet behind MALB, was the three-headed werewolf, with tail wagging.

"Aw, since the curse has been broken, this werewolf acts like a dog again!" said Piper. "I almost feel sorry for the thing. It wants to follow us home."

"Well, one thing is for sure. It won't be going back to Lily Brooke. It may no longer be demonic in nature, but it is still a three-headed werewolf that won't blend into the community very well," giggled Greta.

With that, everyone began laughing at Greta's words. How real they rang true. Lily Brooke had enough demons of its own. The last thing they needed was to bring home a three-headed creature.

"Yeah," laughed Hubert. "That isn't really what I would call lying low. Best to keep these creatures in Lindtzl Kingdom, where the queen can keep them in check."

Magdalena approached the friendly werewolf and gave the top of its head one last pat.

"Stay here, my friend, for the queen, will need you to protect her. We may have won today, but something tells me The Enchanted Forest has more secrets within its depth than we have experienced in our brief time here. Guard the queen with your life, and we will one day meet again."

The werewolf must have understood Magdalena's words as it stayed sitting there at the steel door, still wagging its tail.

Magdalena gave it one last smile and said, "You need a name. How about Skully since in your possessed state, you were going to leave me with the skeletons. We will see you, Skully, when we visit The Enchanted Forest again."

Skully seemed to like his new name, wagging his tail and guarding the steel door at the end of tunnel number two. Hubert was fairly certain that he never wanted to see Skully again, much less ever visit The Enchanted Forest again. But, that was another conversation for another time.

As MALB entered the winter wonderland found behind the steel door, the excitement of finding the large table covered in food became the focus, especially for Hubert. He absolutely couldn't wait to get his hands back on some of the yummy desserts he hadn't had time to taste. Although, he wasn't sure he would ever be able to eat prime rib again for the memories of tonight weren't likely to fade anytime soon.

"Well, Mags, we have completed part A AND part B of your plan. We escaped the castle and defeated the werewolf. Now, how about we focus on part C, getting home?" whispered Gabriel.

"Gabriel, you got it! That is like music to my ears," smiled Magdalena.

The ambiance of the stroll through the winter scenery was breathtaking. Cody, Piper, Greta, Hubert, Gabriel, and Magdalena all reveled at the moment. Christmas was only a week away, and they had all been given the absolute best Christmas gift possible. They had endured the battle with the demonic world, and they had each other. There was nothing more special in life than friends and family, and each one of them knew it.

As they reached the table of food, Hubert dove into the closest seat that he could reach and began stuffing his face. Everyone laughed at the sight and knew the adrenaline he had faced a few moments ago was most likely intensifying his hunger. They all found a seat and decided the third dinner of the evening sounded pretty good.

ENCHANTED GOODBYES

~ Fourteen ~

Sitting at the table, so full they almost couldn't breathe, the friends heard the jingle bells and knew the queen must be arriving. Sure enough, her horse-drawn carriage arrived, and the queen disembarked looking lovelier than ever. MALB could see the happiness in her glow before she even reached the table.

"My children! You have done it! You have saved Lindtzl Kingdom from the evil werewolves! How can I ever repay you?" exclaimed Queen Lindtzl.

"Well, I have an idea," responded Hubert before he gave any thought to what he was about to say.

All eyes turned to Hubert. Secretly, Gabriel was praying that Hubert would somehow find some tact before he spoke again.

"Yes, Hubert? What do you have in mind as repayment?" inquired the queen.

Magdalena's stomach began to drop as she had no idea what Hubert would say next. And the last thing she needed to happen was for him to anger the queen and MALB to be stuck in The Enchanted Forest forever.

"Well, your majesty, I would love to go home. I miss my sleeping bag and my parents. But the problem is, we accidentally discovered this place. I slipped on the snow near the puddle that wasn't frozen and entered this weird vortex that dumped me on a dirt tunnel that led to the spooky forest. Right now, I have no idea how to get back home. I don't have magic, and I'm not a *chosen one*," stated Hubert.

MALB began exchanging glances at each other as Hubert was spilling out their adventures of the evening. His words were blunt, but they were true. None of them knew how to get home. Part C of Magdalena's plan was based upon their experiences up to this point. They had no idea they would meet the queen and no idea how the night would unfold. Now they were left with the impossible task of finding an exit.

"My dear Hubert, do not dismay as I will help you get back home to your family. But, you say you are not a *chosen one*? I thought that I detected a certain vibe from you. Odd, maybe I was mistaken," replied the queen.

Hubert laughed and blurted out, "Me? Oh, goodness, no, I'm the scaredy-cat of the crew. There is no way I would ever be a *chosen one*. I mean, you have to be a wizard or a witch to be one of those. Nope, not me. No flying spells, lily root curses, or golden leaves here, guys."

Hubert wasn't taking the conversation seriously at all, but Magdalena was absorbing every word that was exchanged between the queen and Hubert. Privately, she had wondered if one-day Hubert would find out he was a wizard. His mother was a witch, and his father was a wizard. And apparently, after the last adventure they had Hubert hadn't put two and two together. Hubert was just one of those people that were so self- absorbed, he just didn't think. But Magdalena had thought, *no need to worry him*. If he really were a wizard by birth, the gift of spiritual hearing would manifest itself in the future. Then, he wouldn't be able to deny it. In the meantime, best to let him just be Hubert.

The queen glanced at Magdalena, as she could sense that Magdalena knew Hubert would manifest enchanted abilities. But the queen knew immediately what Magdalena was thinking, based upon her demeanor. And so, the queen played along.

"Yes, Hubert, I'm sorry. My intuition must be off today. It has been quite the night! However, I must thank all of you again for freeing me, freeing my kingdom, and giving me a way to go back to my beloved castle," said the queen.

"Queen Lindtzl, by the way, you have a new guard dog. Well, actually, it is a three-headed werewolf. But don't worry, it is no longer demonic or possessed. His name is Skully, and he is waiting for you by the frozen steel door. He is guarding your castle and has promised to look out for you," smiled Magdalena.

The queen was quite taken aback and uncertain about Magdalena's words.

"I'm sorry, my dear, did you say the three-headed werewolf was now my guard dog?" inquired the queen.

With that, MALB burst into laughter, knowing how odd and insane these words must sound to the queen.

"Yes, mam, when the curse was broken, the werewolf reverted to being a dog, even though it has three heads. It is very submissive and appears to be quite loyal. We named him Skully, as when he was possessed, he was going to leave Magdalena in the cell at the end of tunnel number one to die with all the other skulls and bones inside of the room. I guess it was our attempt of a little humor on a difficult night," explained Gabriel.

"Oh, goodness," laughed the queen. "I see. Well, one thing is for sure, Skully will be very helpful in gathering the kingdom back together. We will need to reach out to all the werewolves and inhabitants of The Enchanted Forest."

Queen Lindtzl knew dawn would be arriving before too long and that she needed to help the children get back to Lily Brooke before their absence was discovered. From underneath her robe, she removed a beautiful snow globe.

The queen held the snow globe up for all of MALB to see. It was a replica of the winter wonderland in which they were all standing. The magnificent scene in the globe showed the table of food, all of them sitting around the table, and having the time of their life.

"I was able to capture one of the most innocent childhood events I have seen in a long time. Here inside of this globe, is my gift to you. May it always remind you of the simple fun and comradery you all equally share. Inside of this globe represents the magic I hope you always feel every year, at the most special time of year. The Christmas gift you have given me may never be matched. You have given me back my home, the one I shared with the king, the one I shall live out the rest of my days inside. My gift to you is the memory of your time in this wonderland. If you ever find yourselves needing anything at all, I am only a globe shake away. This globe is enchanted. Do not break it, my dear children," whispered the queen.

The magic she saw in each of their eyes was worth its weight in gold. The queen was pleased that her gift and touched their hearts. She knew children have a heart of gold. It is the cruel and competitive world that slowly begins to mold them differently as adulthood approaches. This way, she hoped they would always remember the good in everything. It was her eternal gift to them.

"Now, if you ever need me, or you ever want to visit me, simply form a circle around the globe, lay your hands on the top and wish yourselves here. You will find yourselves at this table, and I will find you here," stated the queen.

"How exciting!" shouted Greta. "This is the best gift ever!"

Everyone shouted in unison, agreeing with Greta's sentiment.

"I think Magdalena should keep the globe with her because, without Mags, none of this would have been possible," suggested Piper.

"Agreed!" shouted Gabriel.

Everyone seemed to feel the same way, so Magdalena graciously accepted the gift.

"Thank you, queen, for everything," whispered Magdalena.

"You are most welcome!" responded Queen Lindtzl. "Now everyone come closer to the globe, lay your hands on top of it, and wish yourselves home. Have a very Merry Christmas, and come visit soon!"

MALB approached the globe in Magdalena's hands, and everyone placed one hand on top, closed their eyes, and wished themselves back in Lily Brooke.

CHRISTMAS GIFT

~ Fifteen ~

A few hours later, Gabriel was the first to awaken. He lay there trying to gather his thoughts, a little confused as to where he was at the moment. Remembering the action-packed night, he quickly rolled over to figure out his whereabouts. In front of him was the dwindling campfire that was still putting out a little warmth on this cold, wintery night. He realized he was surrounded by his friends, and everyone was fast asleep in their sleeping bags. Immediately his thoughts went to Magdalena, and he remembered he had woken up last night and found her missing. He crawled out of his sleeping bag and went to Magdalena's.

There on the snow-covered ground, he found her sleeping soundly. She was snuggled down in her pink sleeping bag. He sat down beside her, just watching her sleep, wondering if everything he remembered happening last night was just a dream. He remembered the sound of the werewolves in the night, falling down the slippery slope, the frozen pond, the water puddle, and the wicked vortex, The

Enchanted Forest, Lindtzl Castle, the four tunnels running underneath the enchanted castle, the three-headed beast, the demented tree roots and deep well, and the pit of skeleton bones.

He shivered from head to toe. It was all way too vivid to have been a dream. Then he remembered finding the winter wonderland, Queen Lindtzl, and defeating the beast to break the curse. He laughed to himself as he remembered Magdalena trying to make light of the situation and naming the three-headed werewolf Skully. He then remembered the snow globe, and how the queen had told them to close their eyes and wish themselves home. He looked around and didn't see a snow globe, but he couldn't believe it had all been a dream.

Hubert began to stir and woke up, realized where he was, and sat straight up.

"What happened to us last night?" asked Hubert. "Were we chased by a three-headed werewolf?"

With that, the rest of the gang began slowly waking up in the dawn hours of the morning.

"Yeah, did anyone else dream about being chased by werewolves, or I mean a werewolf with three heads, and trying to escape some crazy booby-trapped castle?" asked Cody.

At this point, Gabriel knew it had not been a dream for the chances they had all dreamed the same nightmare, were about zero to none. He looked up to see Magdalena stretching in her sleeping bag.

As her eyes opened, she saw Gabriel sitting beside her and the remnants of the campfire just behind him.

"Good morning, Gabriel. How did you sleep?" asked Magdalena.

Before Gabriel could respond, Magdalena sat up and pulled her hand out of her sleeping bag.

"What is this?" she asked.

There, inside of her hand, was a snow globe with such a beautiful winter wonderland inside. Looking closer, she noticed six children sitting around a long table adorned in food and desserts. They were laughing and having the time of their lives. Then, it slowly began coming back to her. She remembered waking up to the sounds of the werewolves, or what she had thought was multiple werewolves. She remembered trying to find them in the woods and falling down the slippery slope. She remembered everything that had happened last night.

"Oh, my gosh, this is us inside of the globe!" shouted Magdalena.

Everyone began laughing as Magdalena was the last to join the party, so to speak. *She must have really been in a deep sleep*, thought Gabriel.

"Well, guys, we did it again!" exclaimed Gabriel. "We saved Lily Brooke from the demonic gatekeepers, the three-headed werewolf. We couldn't have done it without teamwork. And as a bonus, we defeated the curse on Lindtzl Kingdom and restored balance to The Enchanted Forest. I'm tired!"

Everyone giggled, realizing it had been quite the evening.

"Mags, thank goodness for your black magic skills. We would have never gotten out that deep well, or survived those wicked tree roots," said Cody.

They all sat around the left-over campfire discussing all the intimate details of their evening, but this time in excitement. For, they had won. They had beaten the curse and saved Lily Brooke and Magdalena from the revenge of the four-legged gatekeepers. Now all they had left to do, was enjoy the holidays.

Christmas was now six days away, and the excitement in each of their eyes couldn't be dimmed. They had survived the last three months, survived the wrath the demons left behind in Lily

Brooke, and had each other. They had made a new friend, found a new land, and strengthened their friendship. What more could they ask for, truly?

"Hey Mags, if you are ready to go home, I will walk you, so you don't have to go alone," whispered Gabriel.

"I would love it, Gabriel," said Magdalena.

Everyone rolled up their sleeping bags, took one last look at the Christmas lights they had used to decorate the old oak tree and tire swing, and went their separate ways.

"Merry Christmas, everyone!" shouted Cody.

"Merry Christmas!" shouted the rest of MALB.

Gabriel and Magdalena headed off towards Gabriel's favorite street in all of Lily Brooke. As they reached Magdalena's house, Gabriel opened the little white, wooden, picket fence gate. He escorted her up the stone steps and to her front door.

"Merry Christmas, Magdalena," said Gabriel.

"Merry Christmas, Gabriel," whispered Magdalena as she softly smiled.

As she reached for a hug, she found his shoulder to be the perfect height. She lay her head on Gabriel's shoulder, closed her eyes, remembering how important his friendship had been in her life, and vowed to never go another three months without her best friend by her side. Thankfulness took over, and a single tear escaped from the corner of her eye.

Gabriel pulled Magdalena from his shoulder, looked her directly in the eye, and said, "Our friendship is the best Christmas gift I could ever receive. You will be my forever friend, Magdalena. I couldn't even imagine life without you."

Magdalena smiled as Gabriel kissed her lightly on the forehead.

"See you soon, Mags," he whispered.

"Very soon," she responded and entered her front door.

Magdalena watched Gabriel turn around and head out the little gate. He turned once more to wave as he headed towards home. She returned the wave, closed the door, and welcomed the smell of cinnamon muffins in the oven. This was going to be the best Christmas EVER!

~ THE END ~

Sneak Peek

Magdalena Gottschalk:

Lindtzl Kingdom

It was the best Christmas ever for Magdalena and her friends. The seasonal festivities those last few days before Christmas had them popping from one holiday party to another. There was singing, laughter, and lots of gift-giving. But for MALB, The Mystical Alliance of Lily Brooke, they knew from first-hand experience that nothing was more important or to be cherished more than friendship.

To date, they had defeated the enchanted demons of Lily Brooke's past and locked them away forever in the enchanted lanterns. Little did they know, the demons had cursed their gatekeeper, the three-headed werewolf, who vowed to revenge their owners' entrapment throwing MALB on the cusp of another whirlwind adventure.

But, Magdalena and her friends pulled together to defeat the hideous beast's curse in the final hours, leaving the friends exhausted yet thankful to return to Lily Brooke. Bound by friendship and loyalty, MALB had survived all the trials the demons had thrown their way. And not only had they survived, but they had made friends along the way.

Defeating the werewolf's curse had led them to the Kingdom of Lindtzl and The Enchanted Forest. Queen Lindtzl herself had been instrumental in helping the children and providing guidance. She had fed them in the winter wonderland and presented them with a coveted snow globe that would allow them to return any time they wanted to visit.

Now that the holidays were past, the friends decided to drop in on Queen Lindtzl for a short visit. She had been so excited to return to her castle upon their departure home. Little did they know the state of affairs had drastically changed since they left the picturesque forest.

MALB finds itself in yet another mystery in The Enchanted Forest. This time, they need to save the queen from the evil forces manifesting upon the kingdom. Will they be strong enough to defeat the evil manipulation, or will they forever be trapped in the hidden kingdom? Stay tuned…

~ Author News ~

M. Gail Grant would like to thank her readers and would kindly ask you to leave a review if you feel inclined to do so! She is very grateful for your feedback and thoughts for future readers.

Join our mailing list to receive periodic updates on new releases, sale information, and local author events:

http://MGailGrant.com
http://www.Facebook.com/MGailGrant
http://www.Twitter.com/MGailGrant
http://www.Instagram.com/MGailGrant

Other Reads by M. Gail Grant:

~ Magdalena Gottschalk: The Crooked Trail

~ Magdalena Gottschalk: Lindtzl Kingdom

Made in the USA
Columbia, SC
28 November 2021